PUFF

CERRIE BURNELL

Wilder
than
Midnight

PUFFIN

PUFFIN BOOKS

UK | USA | Canada | Ireland | Australia
India | New Zealand | South Africa

Puffin Books is part of the Penguin Random House group of companies
whose addresses can be found at global.penguinrandomhouse.com.

www.penguin.co.uk
www.puffin.co.uk
www.ladybird.co.uk

First published 2022

001

Set in 11.5/15.5 pt Georgia
Typeset by Jouve (UK), Milton Keynes
Printed and bound in Great Britain by Clays Ltd, Elcograf S.p.A.

The authorized representative in the EEA is Penguin Random House Ireland,
Morrison Chambers, 32 Nassau Street, Dublin D02 YH68

A CIP catalogue record for this book is available from the British Library

ISBN: 978–0–241–45716–0

All correspondence to:
Puffin Books
Penguin Random House Children's
One Embassy Gardens, 8 Viaduct Gardens, London SW11 7BW

*For Amelie, who fills my heart
with fairy tales.
And my parents, who filled my
childhood with stories.*

Contents

PART TWO: THE SECRETS OF SILVERTHORNE CASTLE

PART THREE: SILVERTHORNE RISING

Faraway
Wood

Aurelia's
Tower

Deep Wood

Wild
Wood

Wolves'
Den

River Spell

Three Bears'
Cottage

Castle

River Spell

Spindle Wood

The Willows' House ↑

Hidden Lake

Deep Wood

Home of the
Forest Folk

Lady
Mal's
House

Wild Wood

Ebony
House

Silverdell
Village

PART ONE

THE WOLVES OF
SILVERTHORNE FOREST

*She slept with wolves without fear, for the
wolves knew a lion was among them.*
R. M. Drake

THE FIRST TALE

The Wolf Child

At the edge of a fathomless forest, in a castle grey as cloud, a baby was born at the stroke of midnight. But, alas, all was not well.

'She's dead,' the young mother gasped, her tumbling hair plastered to her brow, her ragged voice as thin as the curls of smoke snaking their way from the fire as she staggered from her chamber.

Outside in the corridor, her husband stumbled back in shock, grief gripping his heart. He turned away from the tiny bundle, too upset to even gaze upon her.

The mother's eyes burned bright as she crept through the castle, the baby clasped in her arms. A cloak of red velvet thrown swiftly over her shoulders, her feet still bare.

Somewhere a window was open, letting in a snow-laced wind. It skittered through the corridors, carrying away the tiniest whimper, as soft as a nightingale's wing.

Three serving girls huddled together. A golden dog barked in the courtyard. The apothecary, who had helped bring the baby into the world, stood statue still.

The mother hurried on, out into the dancing snowfall. Near the castle's entrance, a trusted huntsman stood alone, keeping watch over the drawbridge. Magnificently tall, shoulders as wide as an ancient oak, his skin the colour of ebony. He was the castle's sworn protector, and he had taken an oath to keep its secrets. All of them.

'She's dead,' repeated the young mother, pushing the little bundle into his arms.

The huntsman took hold of the bundle carefully, taken aback by the pale figure swaying before him in the wind.

A demanding little cry came from within the blankets and a perfect pink foot kicked at the huntsman's elbow.

He gave a smile of relief. 'Look, she's –'

'She will not last the night,' the mother said quickly. 'Take her to the river, bind her to a rock and throw her in. Make sure she sinks to the very bottom. This way is kinder.'

The huntsman peered down and felt his heart still. The babe was as radiant as the winter moon, her hair the silver of stardust, her eyes icy blue. Her right arm, not fully formed, ended in a neat little stump.

She was beautiful, but she had been born with the Mark of the Witch.

The huntsman swallowed his dread and said gravely, 'I will take her away.'

The mother nodded, drew up her scarlet hood and was gone.

Under the watch of the lone pearl moon and a solitary owl, the huntsman rode deep into Silverthorne Forest. Through tangled briars, over shifting rocks and rushing brooks, never pausing. And, as he rode, he sang sweetly to the child, a ballad of sorrow and hope.

For a forest can hold many secrets. Promises murmured beneath a new moon. Pathways so twisted they defy any map. Dark truths hidden in the heart of a wolf. The very air seemed to stir with myth.

The mother's cruel words circled the huntsman's heart. 'She will not last the night.'

We will see about that.

He would have taken the babe home to his own wife and child, raised them as sisters if he could. But he knew news would soon spread of his new daughter, one with stardust hair and the Mark of the Witch. Word would get back to the castle and the child would be put to death. All his family would be in grave danger.

Her only safety lies in the thick of the forest where the Silverthorne wolves reign, and all but a few brave folk fear to tread.

Finally, after riding far into the woods, the huntsman brought his horse to a halt. Tethered her to an ancient ash tree and dismounted in a glade of trembling aspen, and alder buckthorn, still rich with dark berries.

From round his neck the huntsman pulled the garland of lavender he always wore for safety and bent it carefully into the shape of a crown, placing it upon the child's fair head.

Within the forest's folds nearby, a wolf with moonshine eyes awoke and stretched out a long, sinewy limb. Her fur was the bleak white of winter, her teeth sharp, her heart wild. She tilted her snout to the moonlit skies and breathed in the scent of a stranger in her forest. Then she set off at a run. Other wolves were drawn to the sound of her howl, and took up the chase, following their leader.

Soon the gleam of yellow eyes flashed through the dense trees surrounding the alder clearing. Snouts raised to the moon, they sang with a swift, feral yearning.

The wind stirred and the snow whirled. The wolf bleak as winter pawed the earth, glaring hard at the huntsman.

He lowered his gaze in respect and moved towards her. Carefully he laid the child on a bed of leaves at the white wolf's paws.

The huntsman crept back as the wolf put her nose down, taking in the lavender crown's familiar scent.

The baby raised her arms to the wolf, her single hand clasped in a fist. The wolf opened her jaws and tenderly licked the child's cheek, then, slowly, she lay down by the babe in the snow, guarding her from the night. The pack at once surrounding them for protection.

As the wolves' howls continued to ring through the glade a barely noticeable doorway opened and a band of fierce men and women stepped from the dark into the moonlit clearing, drawing their daggers in readiness.

'I have brought this child to the safety of the forest,' said the huntsman, bowing to his friends in solidarity. 'She is already at one with the wolves, and I humbly ask: will you also watch over her?'

The gruffest-looking man pushed his way forward, walking among the wolf pack as if they were family, and peered at the child's luminous hair.

'Where did she come from?' he asked.

'The castle,' the huntsman replied.

The group of Forest Folk muttered among themselves, uncertain, sceptical. They wanted nothing to do with the castle, or its king and queen. But the youngest of them, a girl not much more than a child herself, was drawn to the baby. 'Please,' she murmured to the gruff man, and he saw just how lovely the baby was, and caught sight of her sweet little arm. Gently he took the babe from the wolf's clasp and turned to the huntsman.

'I swear we will protect her,' he said with great solemnness. And the family of Forest Folk welcomed the babe into their home.

And so the huntsman rode away, back towards the Ebony House at the edge of the forest, back to his own wife and child.

And the Wolf Child?

Some say she did not outlive the winter. Others think the wolves devoured her. But there are some who swear that, on nights when the moon is high, they hear her singing.

A voice bright as bone, wild as a wolf. Singing a melody of moonlight and freedom.

CHAPTER ONE

Upon a Dark Horse

Deep in the heart of the forest, a wild-hearted girl rode upon a dark horse. Her hair was as pale as moonlight, and her eyes were the ice blue of the mountains in winter.

She had no light as the wind had stolen her lantern's flame. Yet she galloped on fearlessly, for she knew the paths of the forest as well as the lines that criss-crossed her palm. Trees drew back their boughs to let her pass; stars realigned themselves to light her way. The girl tipped her face to the sky and howled, feral and sweet.

She was wilder than snow on a first winter's morn. Wilder than moonlight on a midsummer's eve. Wilder than midnight in a forest of wolves.

Her name was Wild Rose.

A little way in the distance, the River Spell gurgled like a wise witch's laughter and Wild Rose slowed the dark horse to a canter. A wolf with mottled fur of many shades soundlessly flanked her as she weaved past ancient apple trees, through a glade of winter pines, round a huge dead ash tree, then past a tunnel of hawthorn.

Wild Rose did not even glance at the tunnel, though she caught the bewitching scent of cinnamon and sorrow that drifted from within.

Journeying on, she came to a bend where the river's current calmed to no more than a whisper. The horse and the wolf, named Lullaby for the sweetness of her howl, both halted. Wild Rose leaned into the woodland darkness, sensing a watchful owl high above, a scuffling water rat near the river's edge and somewhere in front a living, wicked solidness.

The Spindle Wood.

Impossible, unfathomable, impassable.

A tangled wall of briar, tall as the trees, laced with thorns as sharp as daggers. No one had ever found their way through it. Carriages and carts from the village took the royal road, which led round it. Nobody ever dared or even dreamed of going through.

Wild Rose dismounted in a smooth, light jump and turned to the stallion. First she stroked his silken mane, darker than jet and woven with ribbons. Then she whispered, with as much authority as she could summon: 'Stay here, Luce.'

He stared at her, black and proud and beautiful. She reached out her arms to him, breathing in a scent that felt like safety.

'I'll be fine,' she assured him, her heart already racing.

Turning towards the thorns, Wild Rose moved forward, a shimmer of hope tingling in her bones.

This will be the night I cross.

Over the years she had mapped and planned and schemed and dreamed that one day she would cross the Spindle Wood and dance in the castle courtyard beyond. It was a pledge she had made often. A pledge made real in dreams and promises.

First she'd had to wait for a night when the clouds were so thick the moon was all but hidden. The forest so dark that no one would notice a lone rider. Not her bright-eyed uncles and aunts, nor the Royal Guard.

Next she'd had to steal the sharpest axe, which belonged to her Uncle Tobias, from the cottage.

Then she'd 'borrowed' the dark horse.

And now here she was. Ready to cross the Spindle Wood.

There was just one thing left. Wild Rose dropped to the earth beneath a young copper beech tree and retrieved a small jar. Her protection spell.

Three thorns from a white rose pushed into three hazelnuts soaked in rainwater and left in the starlight for three nights. Wild Rose bound the little jar to her waist with a length of spider-silk twine and murmured the incantation.

'Thorn of rose, with petal white,
protect my heart on this deep night.
Little nut of hazelwood,
let my path be true and good.
Drop of rain and purest star, guide
me safely near and far.'

Creeping forward, she held her hand out before her. Almost instantly a thorn pierced the skin of her second finger, drawing a droplet of blood. Wild Rose froze, trying to ignore the shooting pain.

Lullaby gave a low growl of caution, but Wild Rose closed her heart to it.

'I'm fine,' she whispered as Lullaby licked the blood from her finger, then she inched cautiously forward again, feeling for the axe at her belt.

Rising to her full height, Wild Rose held the axe high. She sliced and chopped and carved with all the care of a woodcutter, until a hollow had been created, just big enough for one person.

Stepping boldly forward, Wild Rose felt thorns sharp as daggers snare her ragged clothes and matted hair. For a precious moonstruck moment, the Spindle Wood seemed to surrender. But then the maze of thorns began to close in, as if it were swallowing her. Thick, leafy stems twisted and tangled together afresh, catching in her hair, scraping her with thorns, blotting out the moon as they drew her in.

Wild Rose gasped, almost dropping the axe. Behind her Lullaby howled in protest. Suddenly another wolf, pale and fast as lightning, shot from the trees. It swiftly burrowed into the thorns and closed its powerful jaws round Wild Rose's ankle, dragging her free, a handful of thorns still trapped in her hair.

Wild Rose flopped to the ground with a sigh of exasperation as a wolf white as winter and wise as the moon unclamped her jaws and glared at her.

'Fine then, not tonight,' she huffed, glaring at the leader of the wolf pack: Snow.

Snow made no sound, but Lullaby drew back in fear and Wild Rose sprang up and ran over to the dark horse, leaping on to him, her wish for freedom still alive in her heart. The white wolf's eyes burned gold in warning as Wild Rose blew her a kiss before riding swiftly away.

One day she would know the world beyond the woods. One day she would venture into villages or cross the moat to Silverthorne Castle. But not tonight.

Wild Rose galloped away, through the Wild Wood – a stretch of dense woodland on the edge of the forest – and past the Deep Wood, which was known to the villagers as the forest's dark heart. Wild Rose knew it as home.

Lullaby ran by her side, streaking through the trees. Wild Rose kept riding until the scent of lavender in rainwater and burnt arrowroot reached her. This was the sign they were close to the apothecary's house. A place secretly hidden away somewhere between the Wild and the Deep of the forest.

Most homes within Silverthorne had grown weary of arguing and simply become part of the wild. Shrouded in ivy, stained green with moss, or cracked from years of the keening wind. The apothecary's house was so well hidden that it found you, taking you by complete surprise if you stumbled upon it. And, sure enough, the dark horse came to a staircase cut into the ground at steep, jutting angles. Sensing a shift, Wild Rose jerked and gripped Luce's mane more tightly as they crept down the woodland stairway. At its base, an ominous brick wall rose out of the earth, covered in nightshade and fungi and lined with shards of broken glass that glittered cruelly in the starlight.

Wild Rose dismounted, tucked the crook of her right elbow under the horse's chin, into his golden bridle, and led him along the wall, feeling through the mushroom-covered brickwork with her hand. Finally her fingers closed round a devil-horned knocker. But she did not use it. Instead she sank to her knees, poking around in the cold mud until she grasped an iron lever.

She turned to Lullaby. 'I love you, but you can't come in here. Away you go.' She kissed the wolf on the end of her snout and gave her the littlest push.

The wolf gave a growl and Wild Rose bowed her head, pressing their foreheads together, sending her thoughts to the wolf, until Lullaby turned and did as Wild Rose had asked, vanishing away to roam the night country.

Then Wild Rose heaved her full weight on to the lever and held still as the brickwork creaked and shifted until a doorway swung open in the wall. The horse and Wild Rose squeezed through and the door clanged shut behind them.

They entered a long, sweeping garden, a lantern-lit path winding its way to the entrance of a majestic house. It was the colour of bats' wings and had been built so cleverly that the tiles gave the appearance of flowing silk, reaching from the topmost tip of the roof down to the dank earth in one sweep. It was a witch's dream of spires and turrets, and at the centre was a grand tower in which there was a door the shade of pewter.

But Wild Rose never used *this* door, wise as she was to its illusion. Instead she bent down and found a far smaller door tucked almost entirely out of sight. It was at this that she knocked.

There came the gentle patter of soft-shoed feet, a flickering of candlelight and a long, welcoming squeak as the door creaked open and a woman with the elegance of a nightingale stood before her.

The apothecary, Lady Mal, had silky dark hair, rich brown skin, and eyes that seemed to know your thoughts before you even thought them.

'What do you want at this hour, child?'

'To see you, of course.' Wild Rose smiled.

The Lady Mal raised an eyebrow, taking Wild Rose's cold hand and pulling her into the warm. Inside, the ceiling was high, the air dancing with a million dust motes. A fire burned in the hearth with two cauldrons bubbling above it.

The Lady Mal had settled herself in a high-backed chair beside a tall window, eyeing Wild Rose like a cat watching a bird.

'You are too good a thief!' she said musingly. 'I thought we had agreed that you would ask *before* you borrowed my horse.'

Wild Rose shrugged with feigned innocence and the Lady Mal rolled her eyes. 'Well, you're here now. You may as well have tea with me.'

Wild Rose took two fired china cups from a high cupboard, dipping each one carefully into a broth of mint, lemon peel and ginger from one of the cauldrons. It smelled of morning.

'What's bubbling in the other pot?' she asked. It held the aroma of summer wilderness, yet there was an acrid bite to it that stung Wild Rose's eyes. Peeking inside, she saw a huge root of valerian, the white wing of a moth, handfuls of camomile leaves, stems of dried lavender buds and other ingredients she couldn't identify 'Is it a potion?'

The Lady Mal moved to the hearth and gave the pot a stir. 'It is.'

'What does it do?'

Ever since the Lady Mal had spied Wild Rose, aged three, hanging from a tree just beyond her garden, she had welcomed the child to her house to learn the ways of the woods, the knowledge of woodland flowers and the secrets of forest herbs.

Her uncles and aunts might have taught Wild Rose how to cook heart-warming soup, mend and sew her clothes, tell folklore or sing a ballad, but the Lady Mal had taught her everything else. How to chant incantations, how to ride fearlessly and how to stay alive in the bleakest of winters.

Now Lady Mal was quiet for a moment, as if considering her answer. 'It's a sleep potion. Called the Dreamer's Draught,' she said at last.

The Dreamer's Draught.

'To stop nightmares?' asked Wild Rose.

'No, child,' answered the apothecary. 'To send you to sleep for over a hundred hours.' And then, in a much lower voice, she added, 'It can also wipe your memory. The last thing you did before you sleep is forgotten.'

'Will you teach me the recipe?' Wild Rose asked brightly.

The lady held the girl's face in her hands, in an unexpected gesture of tenderness. 'One day I will. One day I will tell you everything I know. But you are too young to learn such dark things today. Come sit with me by the window before I head to the castle.'

Wild Rose took her steaming cup and followed the Lady Mal across the grand room. For this was her other most favourite thing – hearing stories about life in the castle, life in the villages, life beyond the forest.

'Will you take me there one day?' she said with a sigh.

'You know the rules about leaving the forest.' The Lady Mal looked at her pointedly. 'You know it isn't saf–'

'Yes, yes, yes. The villagers think I'm a witch and want to drown me. I'm just sayi–'

Now it was the Lady Mal's turn to cut her off, this time with a look.

'Have you forgotten about the little boy you found by Old Eleena's house?'

Wild Rose fell silent. She had not forgotten. She never would.

✳

It was much later the next morning when Wild Rose finally departed. Back in the forest, the wind whipped up the air, whispering a promise of ice. The black trees stood waiting for that deathly kiss of frost, their long branches clinging to gold leaves with the sorrow of things lost too soon. The day tasted of snow.

Wild Rose began climbing the branches of a weathered elm tree as if its boughs were welcoming arms. Up high, she reached a network of silken twine strung surreptitiously through the treetops. She let a tiny snowflake settle on her tongue before dancing along the hidden wire, her balance so assured you might have believed she had wings.

Far below, Wild Rose saw a figure in a cloak of deepest blue stumbling along the path between the villages of Silverdel and Hazelmere, a heavy basket swinging awkwardly on her arm.

Wild Rose saw villagers in passing all the time, but they rarely saw her as she was forbidden from speaking to them. A rule she only broke if the villager were in mortal danger.

Wild Rose dropped to a crouch, listening hard for the scuffle and snap of her wolves. But she heard nothing. This traveller would not be in any danger as long as she stuck to the path, but Wild Rose watched her all the same, wondering who she was and where she might be headed.

When the girl in the blue cloak turned to gaze at a frozen cobweb, Wild Rose saw she had autumn-brown skin, and wild, springy curls that cupped her face. She seemed young, maybe the same age as her.

The girl paused to examine a fallen birds' nest, peering hard at a little unhatched egg. The outline of a tiny beak that would never sing. Softly the girl blew on the egg, a stream of winter breath, to say goodbye.

She cares for the creatures of my forest, thought Wild Rose, smiling. She kept well back, in case the girl turned her gaze to the sky and spotted her in the trees.

This turned out to be a wise decision for, as the girl moved on, she lifted her face and began to sing. It was a ballad Wild Rose knew, one her uncles and aunts had sung to her since she was a babe. Part of her longed to join in, but instead she listened in wonder as a pair of magpies arced through the sky, circling closer and closer to the singing girl, until one of them landed upon her outstretched arm and she fed it a crumb from her pocket.

She is skilled with birds. Wild Rose marvelled at the girl, wondering again who this blue-hooded stranger was.

Just then a flash of scarlet caught Wild Rose's eye, and she noticed something blood-red and velvety covering the girl's heavy basket.

Red meant only one thing in the forest: danger.

When the blue-hooded girl moved off, leaving the magpies to swoop away, Wild Rose moved too, silently tracking her from the high branches. Sometimes the girl darted off the path to gather late-autumn asters, growing like purple stars on the ground. She lifted her cloak, carefully avoiding the fairies' ring, and crossing with ease over ditches and brooks. She paused to admire another frost-covered spider's web. Wild Rose was intrigued. Most travellers weren't so bewitched by the wonders of the woods.

She kept watching the blue-hooded girl closely, waiting until she stepped from the treeline, near the Hidden Lake, and carried on towards the village of Hazelmere, away from the eyes of prowling wolves and other dangers of the forest.

She is safe.

Then Wild Rose swung herself down to the leafy ground and ran joyfully fast, back through her wintry woods. She didn't need to follow any path, leaping fallen trees and savage thistles, bounding off ivy-covered tree stumps and clusters of thick mushrooms, filling her pockets with the last blackberries of the season, before the frost could take them.

She skirted the silvery trees near the house by the Hidden Lake, glancing across the still waters to a solitary house. A family of cobblers lived here, but they were always out at work, keeping their distance from the depths of the forest, seldom crossing the lake.

She ran on, her chest burning as she sped past an oak tree with a hollow in the shape of a heart, skipped across a forked carriageway, dived in and out of tangleweed and poison oak, her feet so quick she hardly touched the earth.

Bursting into a glade of trembling aspen and alder buckthorn, still rich with dark berries, she came to a halt. On one side of the clearing was a cottage built into the earth, its door low to the ground, hardly noticeable, its windows stained with soot. It looked most unappealing – but then it was supposed to. Its grim appearance hid the wonderful warmth of the cabin within. The home of the Forest Folk.

On the opposite side, concealed behind a bank of thick amber ferns, was another home, this one made of rock and moss. You would never find it unless you knew exactly where to look, and even then its smell might put you off. This was the den of the wolves.

And it was here in this clearing that Wild Rose had grown up. Sleeping among the wolves, singing with her family of Forest Folk.

Wild Rose shoved hard at the tiny window of her family's cottage, tucked her head through it, then somersaulted into the cosy warmth.

Inside, the ceiling was low, and the floor was padded with animal skins. Dried pumpkin, aubergines and squashes with candles flickering within them lit the walls, which were covered in maps.

Wild Rose crawled across the open room and replaced Tobias's axe upon its hook, casting a guilty look towards the tunnels at the back of the room, which led through the woods to the mines and beyond. Her uncles and aunts would be hard at work, digging up jewels for the queen. Tobias would have had to use someone else's axe today . . . She hoped he wouldn't be too cross.

Squeezing back out of the window, she gave a big stretch as tiredness floated over her. Roaming all night with the wolves, meant Wild Rose often slept through the day.

Crossing the clearing, she ducked down to lift the wolf den's layer of ferns, and rolled inside to where her wolves were resting. Tucking her feet up, she snuggled down with Lullaby.

But, just before she fell asleep, an image of the blue-hooded girl wandered through her mind. Wild Rose murmured an incantation for safety, just in case. Then her eyes closed and sleep took her.

CHAPTER TWO

The Girl in the Blue Cloak

Not far from the edge of the forest stood a lone dark cottage. It was a thing of simple beauty, crafted from ebony and draped in curtains of ivy. It wasn't part of the Wild Wood, but neither did it fall within the lanternlight of Silverdel village. It was a place in between; a place that harboured late-night secrets and drew curious looks from passers-by; a gateway between the safe and the wild. Even in midwinter, its garden boasted the drifting scent of lilac and camomile – as if its flowers had turned a magic trick of invisibility.

But the garden had been far from peaceful that morning. Saffy stood in the shade of the pear tree, rocking a screaming baby in a chestnut crib. She was trying to soothe her little brother so her mother Ondina could catch a wink of sleep. But both of their attempts were futile. The baby was furious about being outside, furious about the daylight and furious that Saffy was looking after him.

An ice gust danced past, dragging rough fingers through Saffy's curls and making her laugh then shiver. She searched the sky for a sign of snow, but the morning was clear, cloudless, despite the bitter cold.

We ought to head inside, she thought, drawing herself up and lifting her brother into her arms.

Saffy had hardly taken a step when a bird fell clean from the sky, striking the earth inches from her boot. Clutching the baby in one arm, Saffy lifted the small thing in her hand. A baby raven. It was night-black and so beautiful it was unsettling.

Its pale eyes fixed upon Saffy, then closed forever. The final beat of its heart fluttered in her hands like an omen, and Saffy shivered. On delicate inspection, she found one of its wings had frozen shut. Winter was truly here.

'Mama!' Saffy cried, hurrying inside.

Her mother was there in a moment, taking the raven from Saffy, her face etched with a frown.

'If ravens are dying on the wing, this winter will show no mercy,' said Ondina. 'Run to the village, Saffy. Get bread, buns, milk, cheese and apples from Marla.'

Even though her mother's tone was serious, Saffy's face twinkled with delight. She loved going to the village. Seeing this, Ondina gave her a hard look.

'Get as much as the money will buy – you'll have to haggle hard. I mean it, Saffy – don't go buying buttons or lace or any such nonsense.'

Saffy nodded her head with serious concentration as her mother took the wailing baby from her and bundled Saffy into a dark blue cloak. Its hem was caked with mud, its wooden toggle worn slim by the press of many fingers.

'Once you have all the food, I need you to go to your grandmother's house.'

Saffy's eyes became starry bright in amazement. 'On my own?' she breathed.

Living at the foot of the forest, Saffy had met many a lost traveller who had stayed in the woods too long and come stumbling to her parents' door, shaking with fright. Some whispered of sharp-toothed wolves, others of small men and women with dagger-sharp axes; some spoke of the Witch of the Woods.

Once a man had come in, his hair wild, his face shining with wonderment. 'There's a phantom in this forest,' he had proclaimed. 'A girl who can fly and dance through the trees.'

Saffy was never afraid of these curious, story-weaving folk. Her mother refused to turn anyone away, no matter how late or early the hour, and Saffy had seen how easily a cup of nettle tea could soothe a fractious soul. She knew the light and dark of the forest.

But never had Saffy made the trip to her Grandma Eleena's house alone.

A silence coated the cottage in the pause that followed Saffy's question. A silence made of a million threads of motherhood that linked their two hearts.

Ondina looked at her daughter and nodded. Saffy stood still, awestruck by the responsibility.

'You remember the rules?' asked Ondina crisply.

'Yes,' Saffy answered diligently.

When I see a wolf, still my heart but keep moving.

Always stay calm. The wolves won't attack if I'm not afraid.

Never set foot in the forest without lavender – just in case.

Saffy had seen wolves many times – most of the villagers had. But Saffy had been lucky enough to be perched on her father's shoulders as he held out lavender to them, seen how at ease they were with him, learned how to move slowly through their territory without causing alarm.

Her father had once served at the castle. There was no better huntsman in all the land, yet he never harmed the wolves. On many occasions, when Saffy had taken her father his lunch on the cusp of the Wild Wood, she'd spotted a wolf and softly walked by it. But always with pockets stuffed with lavender.

'You need to leave by mid-morning. Go straight through the Wild Wood, don't stray from the path and stay at Grandma Eleena's till Papa comes to get you,' said Ondina, kissing Saffy's forehead while the baby crossly squirmed.

Saffy dashed to the village, vaulting lightly over the gate that marked the beginning of the village, the empty basket swinging on her arm.

The path that led through Silverdel was cobblestone and Saffy stomped her way along it, the navy cloak dragging on the ground, catching on loose stones and making her trip. She wished she could discard the bothersome cloak, but the air was freezing. Folk bustled round her in buttoned-up coats and dark wool scarves, crinkling their eyes into smiles when they saw her. Saffy beamed back.

A little goat butted Saffy's legs and she giggled, gently pushing the hungry creature away. Then a flash of deep violet caught her eye and Saffy stopped quite still.

Most of the folk of Silverdel were dressed in the colours of autumn. Deep greens, fading yellows and soft nut browns, with a hint of orange if you were lucky, or a rare peacock feather tucked in a cap. But here was a girl in a cloak the hue of midnight tulips.

Saffy gasped. She had never seen anything so glorious in all her twelve years. Who could it possibly belong to? Then she realized – she should have known. There was only one person who might own such a garment: Verity Silkthread.

Saffy felt her heart sink with resentment. Verity was beyond pretty. Her skin a perfect black, her tightly coiled hair woven into such elaborate braids she was the envy of everyone in Silverdel. But it wasn't her beauty that bothered Saffy, or the fact that Verity behaved as if she herself were the queen. It was that Saffy was soon to become Verity's assistant or, to put it less politely, her 'serving girl' when Verity began attending the castle.

Working at the castle was something Saffy should have been excited about. It was what every village girl hoped for – to venture to a place unknown, secretive, almost forbidden. To grace the same corridors and ballrooms as the royals. And Saffy might have been excited too, but she didn't trust Verity, not one bit.

'Good day, Saffron,' came the too-sweet voice as Verity spotted her.

'Hello, Verity. I love your cloak,' Saffy gasped, reaching out in adoration.

'Don't touch it! It's not for you.' Verity snorted, her braids dancing round her heart-shaped face. 'It's royal velvet! It was a gift to my mother from the queen herself.'

'For her teeth,' said Saffy without thinking.

Verity's face hardened to a dangerous scowl. 'For her talents!' she almost spat.

'Of course!' Saffy said, bobbing a curtsy by way of apology and almost tripping over the hem of her blue cloak in her hurry to depart.

Though Verity was the envy of the village, the true beauty was Verity's mother, Arabelle. Arabelle's face could have set a thousand hearts aflame, and Queen Evaline had been quick to notice the radiant smile of her most talented seamstress.

None of the villagers could forget the day Arabelle returned from the castle, puffy-eyed and swollencheeked. None forgot the terrible sound of her sobbing. Her teeth all removed, replaced with white marble ones that rattled and chattered whenever she spoke. It was Ondina, Saffy's mother, who had stepped in and offered remedies for the pain, and words of encouragement and healing. It was Ondina who had restored Arabelle's courage. And it was because of this kindness that Arabelle had arranged for Saffy to attend the castle with Verity.

It was such a gracious offer, Saffy's family could hardly say no, even though they would have preferred her to stay clear of such a place. And more coin could never go amiss in a house on the brink of Silverthorne Forest.

The scent of honeyed buns and baked currants reached Saffy through the cold. She flitted in through the open door of the bakery and breathed in happiness. On the counter were plates of creamy pastries, apple turnovers, sultana bread and slices of winter cake full of glistening cherries. Even though Saffy knew she had to buy buns and savoury loaves for her grandma, she could not help longing for a warm cinnamon swirl.

'Morning, young Saffy,' cooed Marla from behind the counter. She was a mother to six sturdy sons, and the embodiment of the life-affirming comfort of cake.

'Hello.' Saffy smiled shyly.

'These for your lovely mum?' asked Marla as Saffy handed her the coins and told her what they needed.

'My grandma,' Saffy answered, pretending not to notice the hush that ran round the small hot room.

Not all the villagers believed in the unlikely tale of an old woman and her son living in the depths of the blackened forest – a place where unwanted children were left to perish, a place of wickedness and whispers. They thought it no more than a myth. Others knew better than to doubt it.

Saffy thanked Marla, gathered up her laden basket and wandered back towards the village gate, clutching the delicious cinnamon swirl Marla had tucked on top of her order. Saffy could not keep from grinning.

'Now where are you going, little Saffron?' A voice sweeter than blackberries drifted through the frosty air.

'To my grandma's,' said Saffy, warily turning to face Verity again.

'Won't you be cold? They say there's snow on the way.'

Saffy shook her head, and tried to leave – but her eyes drifted to the fabric bundle bound up in Verity's arms. It was velvety and scarlet, like midwinter wine or the fallen petals of a rose.

'Wouldn't you like to try on one of my old cloaks?' Verity simpered, and Saffy found herself forgetting the cinnamon swirl, lowering her basket to the cobbled stones, stepping out of her plain blue cloak and slipping into one of crimson glory.

Saffy recognized it as the cloak Arabelle had made her daughter two winters past. It was now too small for Verity, but just the right size for Saffy.

The splendour was instant. The hood was fur-lined and the plush velvet sweeping down to Saffy's ankles felt like a ball gown.

Verity tucked a little springy curl behind Saffy's ear. 'It really suits you,' she said genuinely.

'It's ever so lovely,' Saffy said with a sigh, unconsciously gripping the red velvet.

Verity grinned and handed her a wax-sealed letter. 'Do you know the Willows' shop in Hazelmere?' she asked smoothly.

Saffy nodded. Everyone knew it: they were the most esteemed cobblers in the kingdom.

'I need you to pay a visit.'

'Hazelmere's a little out of my way,' said Saffy uncertainly.

Verity was heartsore for Jack Willows. And Jack would do whatever she wished. Everyone knew it, yet Verity's parents forbade their love and intentions to marry.

Her mother, Arabelle, had not given up her perfect teeth for nothing. Verity, when she turned sixteen, was to be married to the queen's favourite nephew, who lived in a distant kingdom of mountains and snow. But Verity, with her heart on fire, would burn the whole forest down if it meant she got her way.

'If you deliver this letter into Jack's hands, you can keep the cloak.'

Saffy almost fell over with astonishment. 'F-f-forever?' she stuttered.

Verity stooped so her eyes were level with Saffy's. 'If you don't mind returning tomorrow for the reply.'

Saffy nodded and the two girls looked at one another, each lost in their own wonder at what this could mean.

Who might Saffy become in a cloak like this? Who might Verity be if she were allowed to marry the boy she loved?

'But what reason could I use to go to the Willows' shop?' Saffy asked nervously, her heart already fluttering.

'Say I sent you,' Verity said with a chuckle. 'That I wish Jack to design a pair of shoes for me to wear to the Midwinter Ball. Shoes that look like they're made from ice.'

'The Midwinter Ball,' Saffy murmured. 'It's in nine days – will there be time?'

Verity looked at her knowingly. The Midwinter Ball was the greatest celebration in all the land, and this year's was to be especially grand as the king and queen were looking for a young man to take their daughter's hand in marriage.

As a single snowflake drifted down from the clouds, Saffy boldly nodded.

And so a promise was made on a winter's morn and, as the first snow fell, a girl walked into the wolf-wild woods with a letter and a scarlet secret.

CHAPTER THREE

The Scarlet Cloak

The path that led into the forest was wide and clear at first. Trees slanted back as if in welcome and birdsong trilled through the air. Snow had not yet reached the Wild Wood. Beneath Saffy's feet, the mud was dry.

She stroked the scarlet bundle tucked on top of her basket. She didn't dare wear it yet, in case someone from the village spotted her and word got back to Ondina. Her family owned nothing as dazzling as this in their entire home.

A crow cawed high above and Saffy's heart fluttered. Somewhere between the rising fir trees and the moss-covered oaks, her father, Bow, was chopping wood. If Saffy paused for long enough, she might even hear the distant ring of his axe, but she wasted no time.

The wide track soon became a muddy lane, curving in unexpected places like the trail of a curious snake. Saffy followed it exactly, gathering landmarks in her mind as she went.

A tree with a hollow in the shape of a heart. A rotten log laced with a frill of angel-white mushrooms. A fallen sparrows' nest with a single cracked egg still inside. On impulse, Saffy crouched down and blew on the little egg as a final farewell.

Two sleek-winged magpies arced through the air and Saffy called them down with a song, feeding them little crumbs and currants, admiring the iridescent gleam of their feathers. She loved all birds, but magpies were her favourite.

The lane looped in a very small perfect circle, just big enough for a child to stand inside, and, just as she raised her foot, something made Saffy pause. There were many rumours and rhymes about Fae circles to be heard in the village of Silverdel. Tales and songs of unsuspecting children falling prey to the spiteful nature of fairies, and ending up drowned or blind or bald.

Saffy hesitated a moment, listening to the breath and beat of the forest. Her mother had told her not to believe the nonsense she heard in the village. That the Fae were bright-hearted, intelligent creatures who did not cause unnecessary harm. Even so, like all the villagers, Saffy had grown up fearing the wicked fairy Dormevega.

She tried to put the Fae far from her mind. As she walked on, frost-bitten nettles stung Saffy's ankles and spiky ferns scratched sourly at her cheeks. The trees bore down upon her like an angry huddle of wizards. A soft whisper of doubt began to curl round her heart. Had she taken the right path? Did she really have time for such an errand?

She started parting the leaves, forcing her way through the trees, the scarlet cloak in the basket giving her courage. But it was as if the forest had made itself into a wall. Saffy pushed harder with both her hands and, with a clipped snapping, the leaves gave way and she tumbled into stark daylight, landing by a lakeshore gilded with winter. With a sigh of relief, Saffy dropped the basket, staring in awe, then cursed as a currant bun fell out and rolled away. Before her was the house by the Hidden Lake and in the misty distance behind it was the village of Hazelmere.

The lone house stood proud, and a few quiet swans eyed Saffy from the lake. A mallard quacked in disapproval and a red squirrel gave her a startled glance before fleeing.

Saffy skirted the lake, skipped by the house and hurried into the village.

Hazelmere was a lot larger than Silverdel, the River Spell churning its way rapidly through it. The first fine layer of fallen snow had been trampled away by the tread of boots and stamp of many hooves. The atmosphere was different here too – livelier, merrier. Everyone seemed to own a fabulous winter bonnet or have a pack of hunting hounds barking at their heels, and the air was scented with cocoa and clementines.

Saffy felt uplifted by everything she saw. A choir singing sweetly in the village square. Carriages gilded with gold. Wreaths of pressed flowers decorating shop doorways.

She dashed on, trying to avoid horses draped in finery or children playing near the riverbank, longing for it to freeze so they could skate on it. She winced as she passed a butcher's shop full of feathered birds. Crossing a wide wooden bridge over the roughest bend of the river, Saffy breathed in the delicious smell of roast chestnuts, before hurrying down a winding path and arriving at the most famed cobblers in all the land: the Willows.

The scarlet cloak is mine.

Saffy trembled with delight. But she hadn't delivered the letter yet; she couldn't let herself get so easily carried away.

Stepping inside, she was overwhelmed by chatter and welcome. Even though the shop was bustling with people, Benjamin Willows gave her a vast smile.

'Hello, Miss Hunter,' he grinned, tipping his cap.

'Hello,' Saffy murmured back, trying not to blush as the room swivelled its gaze to her. She shrank awkwardly inside her old dark blue cloak.

'What can we do for you?'

Saffy tried not to sound nervous, but her voice was still whisper soft. 'I have a request for a commission,' she mumbled. Benjamin raised a cheerful eyebrow at her, thinking it must be for Ondina or Bow. 'For the Midwinter Ball,' she said quickly.

Benjamin nodded. 'Something fancy?'

'Very fancy and very fabulous,' Saffy said in a rush.

'I'll fetch Jack,' Benjamin said warmly. 'He's much better at all that intricate detail than me.'

Moments later, Jack appeared behind his father, his gaze a little distant, his manner aloof. And Saffy was reminded why almost every girl, and some of the boys, in the village were sweet on him. He was tall and willowy, his long dark hair falling over his face as his soft green eyes peered out a little curiously.

Ordinarily Saffy would have had nothing to say to the village heart-throb, but the thought of the scarlet cloak gave her courage.

Jack approached and knelt calmly before her, ready to take the measurement of her foot, and Saffy suddenly felt overwhelmed.

'They're not for me – the ice slippers. They're for Miss Silkthread,' she hastily explained.

Jack raised his head, his green eyes flashing with a sudden alertness, his face lit with a soft smile. And Saffy realized he must still care very much for Verity.

'*Ice* slippers?'

Saffy nodded apologetically, aware of the room watching her and feeling her neck turn hot.

Jack cocked his head. 'Like a skate?'

'More like something . . . magical,' Saffy said – and quickly thrust Verity's letter at Jack. To Saffy's immense relief, he casually took the letter and tucked it into his pocket. 'A shoe that looks like . . . ice.'

'I don't know about ice,' Jack pondered with a frown. 'But maybe . . . glass?'

Sensing he was already busily thinking up designs for the girl he still loved, Saffy turned to leave. But as she moved past Jack her basket tipped, almost spilling out the red cloak.

Jack went to catch it, then frowned. 'Is that Miss Silkthread's old cloak?' he asked as if it had stirred a memory.

Saffy could not keep the smile from her face. 'No,' she replied, almost giddy with joy. 'It's *my* new cloak!' And she bounded away.

Dashing back through Hazelmere towards the forest, the day seemed full of wonders. A mirror-thin film of ice was already gleaming on the surface of the Hidden Lake and the wind whirled with flurries of snowflakes. Saffy spun round, making certain that no one was watching, then threw the heavy blue cloak off and twirled into the scarlet cloak, feeling its warmth embrace her.

She could have danced with glee. But instead Saffy dropped to her hands and knees and inched towards the lake's half-frozen surface. Placing one hand then the other upon the ice, she gazed down at her reflection, the scarlet hood flowing round her shoulders like the cowl of a queen.

What would her family think of such an extravagance? And how would she explain where she got it from?

I'll hide the cloak at Grandma's house, Saffy thought with a mischievous grin.

Suddenly something dark moved beneath the ice's surface, causing Saffy to startle. She stood up quickly, only now remembering Ondina's warning to be quick. The sky above her was already turning to grey and it occurred to Saffy that she didn't know the time. Glancing at the pale sun, she realized the journey to the Willows' shop had taken her much longer than she'd hoped.

Never mind. I'll dash straight to Grandma's.

She scooped her basket up, grabbed the hem of the scarlet cloak and ran round the lakeshore, back into the woods. Past the Fae circle, round the fallen nest, but the little cracked egg was now gone. Over the decaying log she went, which was now covered in red mushrooms. Strange.

Look for the hollow-heart tree, she told herself. Yet the tree did not appear. Nor did the wider track that curled away into a grove of larch trees and on towards her Grandma Eleena's cottage.

'Never mind, I'll go back to the lake, start again.' Saffy turned on her heel, keeping her footfall light, her mind spinning with thoughts of a new ruby-red life.

But, when the lake did not emerge, Saffy felt the slightest ruffle of alarm. She forced down the worry and settled herself on a tree stump, speaking out loud in a tone that echoed her mother's.

'I can always find my way in the forest.'

But, as she said this, something else came to her. A lost memory floated through Saffy's mind like a song she couldn't quite remember the words to:

Never wear red in the Silverthorne wood,
Not crimson, nor ruby
Or any such hood . . .

Saffy shivered. She was sure she must be getting the words mixed up. But all the same.
I need to keep moving.
She drew the hood more tightly round her ears, closed her eyes and consulted the map of her soul. Her father was somewhere chopping firewood. The apothecary, Lady Mal, was rumoured to live out deep in the forest, beyond the gaze of watchful eyes. Saffy's grandmother's home was nestled just round the corner, on the other side of the Deep Wood. All she had to do was find it. She ate half a small bread roll for reassurance, though it was part-frozen and tasted strangely of sadness.

Saffy stood up with a new sense of purpose and walked on. On and on she paced, her boots wet and slippery, the basket heavy at her elbow. She refused to worry; soon enough she would be snug beside her grandma's hearth. It was only when the wind bit harder and the light began falling faster than the snow that a shadow of real fear slid over Saffy. The forest at night was no place for a child, not even one who understood its dangers.

She put the basket down and sighed wretchedly, clinging to the cloak. Maybe she should turn back. She knew the vague direction of Silverdel. But what would her mother say of her lateness? And what would become of her grandma and her Uncle Wilf if she didn't deliver the basket of food?

'I have to find Grandma's cottage,' she said out loud.

A branch snapped in the falling dusk. Against her own will, Saffy turned, her view partly obscured by the swathe of fur that lined her hood. But there was no mistaking what she saw: a creature crafted from menace and grace.

A striking bone-white wolf.

CHAPTER FOUR

Wild Rose

Saffy felt her heart tremble, her mouth open in a gasp. 'Beautiful,' she heard herself whisper.

The creature was a long way from her, its eyes lantern bright.

It's just a wolf, she told herself, gripping the basket to steady her.

The white wolf peeled back its lips and gave a soft moan. Saffy blinked in surprise, keeping her step even, her movements controlled as she crept away. She hardly looked where she was going as she listened for the rasp of the wolf's breath, the crackle of leaves beneath its feet. The wind mercilessly stole sounds from her ears, stinging her eyes and tugging furiously at her hair. The path dipped and twisted and Saffy pressed on, not daring to stop.

The wolves won't attack if you're not afraid.

Risking a glance behind her, Saffy could see two luminous eyes still following her through the trees. Her blood almost turned to ice. The gap between her and the wolf was now a measure of hope rather than distance or time.

Lavender.

It was her father's voice in her mind. Saffy dropped the basket, startling both the wolf and herself, as she reached into her cloak pocket. It was silken and completely empty but for half a stale roll. A thin sweat broke over Saffy's forehead. The lavender was in her blue cloak. Her blue cloak discarded by the lakeside . . . She had no protection.

The wolf gave a brisk howl. Saffy felt her throat begin to close and she lurched backwards, almost falling. Whirling in the opposite direction, abandoning the basket, she pleaded with herself not to run. It was the worst thing she could do.

But something in her soul raged against her shaking bones and she fled.

All around her, the wolf's cry was met with others.

A hunting *pack*.

Saffy hurled herself off the path, panting hard as sweat streaked her skin. She plunged into a snarl of branches. Roots snatched at her, brambles bit like teeth, but Saffy continued to fling herself forward.

I do not want to die in the woods.

How far was she from the village, from the lake, from her grandmother's? How far had she strayed from the path?

A desperate wail escaped her lips. 'Grandma! Grandma, help me!' she shrieked. 'Daddy, Daddy! Save me, please . . . Lady Mal! Anyone! Please help!'

But there came no answer. Only her own voice thrown back by the wind.

The wolves seemed to be everywhere: in front, beside, behind her . . . Saffy forced herself to stop. Trembling, she turned, staring defiantly through her tears. She hadn't even known she was crying. Stealthily the wolves moved closer.

In desperation, she pulled the bread roll from her pocket and threw it, distracting the white wolf for a heartbeat. And, in that moment, a burst of light blinded her. Saffy swerved to the side as a wild-eyed girl shot out of the branches, her tiny lantern spilling its glow over both of them. Saffy gasped in shock.

'Give me your cloak,' the girl demanded.

'No!' Saffy sobbed, clinging to the cloak in confusion. Was this strange girl really going to rob Saffy and then leave her to die by the jaws of the wolves?

'I won't hurt you,' said the girl. She looked young but was tall and gangly-limbed. In the light of the lantern, her bare feet were stained green as moss.

Saffy's breath quickened, coming out in hard, broken rasps. The girl glanced at the wolves, quite unafraid.

'That's enough now!' she snapped at them, as if they were a band of drunken thieves.

Saffy blinked in amazement as the pack halted, tilting their snouts to the far-off moon and howling wildly.

As the girl turned back to her, Saffy almost cried out. For in the place where her right hand should have been there was nothing. Her arm ended just below the elbow, in a neat little stump. Saffy had heard of such things. The villagers would have called it the Mark of the Witch.

A girl, all alone. Yet she is not afraid of the wolves. Is she the phantom of the forest?

The girl leaned forward, staring straight at Saffy. 'Wolves love red. Give me your cloak and I will save your life!'

Saffy groaned as the half-sung memory stirred fully within her.

> *Never wear red in the Silverthorne wood,*
> *Not crimson, nor ruby*
> *Or any such hood.*
> *When wolves go a-hunting,*
> *They only see red.*
> *And if you wear scarlet,*
> *You'll soon end up dead.*

Regret stung Saffy hard. How could she have forgotten? How could she have been so stupid?

She flung the cloak off, trembling at the restless howls of the wolves, the hunting pack seeming to draw closer. The forest girl straightened up, seized the cloak and twirled it round her shoulders, fastening it before Saffy had time to breathe.

She held out her little arm to Saffy, the lantern aglow on the end of it, its wicker hook hanging over the crook of her elbow. 'Take the light.' The girl smiled encouragingly.

Saffy took in the ice-blue eyes, the matted moon-bright hair, her quirky grin. She seemed to have too many teeth, all jumbled upon one another. And all at once Saffy trusted this girl with her life. She reached out and grabbed the lantern, lifting the wicker hook off the girl's little arm, not at all afraid as her fingers brushed the stump.

'Are you a witch?' Saffy whispered.

The girl giggled softly. 'No, I'm Wild Rose.'

'I'm Saffron . . . I live near Silverdel.'

'You're far from home,' Wild Rose said sternly. 'Wait till the pack has gone, then take the path by the fallen willow. It's a long way, but it will lead you back to Silverdel by morning. Do not run and do not stop.' Then she pulled a sprig of lavender from within her tangled hair and pushed it into Saffy's hands.

'Thank you,' Saffy gasped, but Wild Rose turned and was gone, and the wolves with her.

The wind stirred, reminding Saffy of how cold she was, especially now she had no cloak at all to protect her. Clasping the lantern tightly, she turned to the deep dark forest in a shocked stupor and walked on. She knew not for how long, but after a time another rhythm came slowly to her. Saffy stood very still, realizing it was the beating hooves of a horse.

Who would be out riding at this late hour?

She drew back abruptly as an enormous horse burst from the trees, rearing up at the sight of the lantern. Saffy leaped clear of the creature, skidding into a heap of frozen blackberry bushes, her heart startling painfully.

The stallion was huge, its coat the colour of a starless sky.

'Easy, easy,' came a lilting command. The horse lowered its hooves, pacing in agitation, nostrils flaring. 'Come now, Lucifer. Hush,' said the rider soothingly.

As Saffy stared at the midnight stallion, her mouth fell open. For there was the gleaming bridle of gold, the mane twined with colourful silk, the sleek, saddleless coat. *The Lady Mal.*

Most of the villagers would have crossed themselves or run for their lives. But Saffy knew that Lady Mal was not to be feared.

Sliding from the horse's back, the Lady Mal laid a soothing hand on the horse's thick neck, a stillness radiating from her.

'What in the name of the goddess are you doing out in the woods, Saffron?' Her tone was like ice.

'Lady Mal,' Saffy whimpered, flinging herself into the apothecary's arms. The Lady Mal wiped Saffy's tears away with her cape. 'I was going to my grandma's house . . . I got lost.'

'You got lost,' said the Lady Mal, each word a tiny, sharp-edged flake freezing Saffy's heart.

Saffy swallowed, trying to keep the truth from spilling out of her. 'I-I-I . . . was delivering a letter on my way,' she stuttered, careful not to mention the scarlet cloak. 'It wasn't the usual route.'

Wolf song rose through the woods and the Lady Mal touched a garland of lavender at her throat.

'There was a girl,' Saffy blurted out. 'She saved me. She gave me her lantern. A girl with one hand.' The hint of a smile softened the Lady Mal's face. She swept Saffy into her arms and seated her swiftly on the horse's back, swinging up behind her.

'I'm sure there was,' she breathed, 'but let's get you home before the wolves are upon us.'

Saffy nodded, gratefully leaning in and weaving her fingers through the mane of the magnificent horse.

The Lady Mal clicked her tongue and the horse galloped away.

Saffy forced herself to stay alert as the horse charged on, plunging off pathways Saffy didn't recognize, finding routes that looped and tangled through impassable thickets, skirting clearings and groves she'd never known, crashing through a stream dappled with lights, though Saffy could see no lanterns.

She was almost delirious with exhaustion, yet she saw things that she was sure could not have simply been dreams. A woman like her grandma stepping from the bark of a tree. An odd little cottage cut into the roots of the forest, its chimney a blackened tree stump. A child alone in a clearing, sharpening an axe over a glowing fire. Or was it a small man? Glancing up, Saffy saw a gilt-edged mirror hung in the boughs of a sycamore tree.

The horse halted very suddenly, jolting her from her reverie. Saffy whimpered as it whinnied and stamped, its breath pouring out like steam.

'Hold on tight,' the Lady Mal soothed, completely composed. Then the horse was leaping, soaring, flying over a gap of some sort.

The stallion's hooves skidded over deep snowfall, slowing and lurching dangerously. Lady Mal gripped Saffy tightly as the night became paler, the sky huger, and together they broke through the treeline and bolted unevenly towards the halfway house that was her home, slush kicking up around them in arcs of frosted silver.

'Saffy!' Her name rang through the air, then Ondina was pulling her daughter from the horse. 'Saffron. Saffron.' She turned to a group of anxious villagers who stood at the edge of the forest, each of them bearing torches, making the woods look fierce. 'Tell her father she's here. We've found her – she's home.' Ondina's voice was a wisp of smoke in her cracked throat.

'I got lost.' Saffy was sobbing, shivering uncontrollably.

Ondina ran her hands over her daughter's face, through her knotted curls.

'Did anything hurt you? Anyone?' Ondina asked, her voice thin with exhaustion.

Saffy shook her head. 'No. A girl saved me. A girl with one hand. A girl called Wild Rose.'

Ondina sank down, pulling Saffy with her. A look of awe was on her face. 'She saved you from the wolves?'

'Yes.' Saffy sniffed. Her mother laughed then, quite unexpectedly, as she held her daughter close, kissing Saffy's dark curls.

'Then you both have lived because of your father's courage,' she murmured.

Saffy had no idea what this meant, but she was too worn out to wonder.

'Let's get you inside.' Ondina sighed, smiling gratefully at the Lady Mal. 'It'll soon be midnight.'

As the cry went up through the dark trees that the missing girl was home, Saffy let herself be briskly ushered inside. The warmth of a steady fire burning in the hearth hit her first, its flames leaping hypnotically. Then she realized that the room was rather full.

Verity was in the corner fretfully weeping, her mother Arabelle hovering beside her. And across the other side of the room Saffy spotted the entire Willow family leaning against the wall, faces masked in shadow.

'Why are they here?' Saffy asked quietly.

'They were worried for your safety,' Ondina muttered, nodding to the two families as she led Saffy across the room to the ladder-like staircase and hurried her upstairs.

'Let's get you warm, my love,' Ondina sighed, leaving Saffy to strip off her wet clothes and scrub herself in a small tub of hot water. Then she pulled on a nightgown and gathered many blankets before tiptoeing back downstairs.

Saffy's father, Bow, sat at the table, the baby asleep in his arms. He stood and kissed Saffy roughly on the top of her head, sighing with relief at the sight of her. Ondina was perched in the sewing chair, a little rosiness rising in her cheeks as she sipped warm whisky.

The Willows and the Silkthreads faced each other silently. Verity's eyes trained on Jack, Jack staring numbly at the floor. The Lady Mal stood near the fire, an authority to her stillness. And outside by the window the horse Luce chewed and whinnied contentedly.

Even with the strange scene before her, the whole house felt steeped in soft serenity, like the moment you wake from a nightmare and realize it's no longer true. As Saffy peered round the room, the mood shifted. Every eye was turned upon her again, apart from Verity's.

On the table lay the letter Saffy had delivered to Jack that very afternoon. The wax seal broken, Verity's neatly inked hand there for all to see. Beside the letter was Saffy's blue cloak, crumpled and damp with snow.

'As soon as the wolves started to howl, I knew something was wrong,' Ondina began.

Saffy perched nervously beside her father, who drew her gently into his arms alongside her grumpy baby brother, as her mother continued.

'I told myself it was the suddenness of snow,' Ondina said. 'But my heart would not heed the lie.' She turned her owl-like gaze to Verity's mother, Arabelle.

Arabelle, the beauty of the village, with her radiant black skin and neatly coiled hair, took up the story. 'It was only because of the cold that I went down to the cellar to fetch a blanket for a neighbour's child. I wasn't even looking for a cloak or cape.' Her tone was sweet, but edged with something perilous. 'Then I noticed a trunk at the back of the room had been left open, and I found that one of the garments from my daughter's dowry was missing.'

Verity gave a moan. 'I didn't know it was *that* important.' Her voice was as small as a mouse's, but Arabelle rounded on her, her face drawn tight.

'I have sacrificed so much for you!' Arabelle growled to her daughter and the room went still. 'That red velvet was given to me by the queen. It was a gift like no other . . . Do you think it was just a token for you to give away?'

'Saffy knew better than to accept such a gift,' said Ondina sternly. 'When Arabelle came to my door, I foolishly did not believe her. That is until Benjamin Willows arrived, holding our blue family cloak, found discarded by the lake.'

'What happened, Saffy?' Bow asked softly.

'I delivered the letter for Verity and put on the scarlet cloak. I forgot the warning, Father. I'm so sorry . . . A white wolf followed me. Then more came.' Saffy tried not to lose herself in the memory, forcing herself to keep talking. 'I got scared and I ran. But a girl with one hand saved me.'

Bow stared at her very intently, clutching the baby to his chest.

'She took the scarlet cloak from me, and drew the wolves away.' Saffy gulped, overwhelmed by the thickening stillness in the room. 'Then the Lady Mal found me and brought me here.'

'You gave the cloak to a beggar?' It was Verity who spoke, her voice full of anguish.

'She's not a beggar. She lives in the woods – I've seen her.' The room swivelled like a spun dagger to stare at Jack Willows. 'Two winters ago, when Joel fell in the lake, a girl with one hand appeared from the trees and pulled him out.'

The adults exchanged quick, fleeting glances.

'A child who lives in the forest?' asked Arabelle.

'I think she lives with the wolves,' said Saffy.

Arabelle gazed curiously at the Lady Mal. 'Is she some sort of witch? A sorceress? Is she the Wolf Child?' Under her breath, she muttered to Verity, 'We can kiss that cloak goodbye forever.'

'No,' answered the Lady Mal with a bewitching smile, and she glanced at Ondina who gave a subtle nod and rose to her feet.

'You'd better all sit down,' said Ondina. 'It's time for another tale. And let it be known that every word spoken here tonight remains within these walls.'

CHAPTER FIVE

The Lost Babe

espite the late hour and the tension in the air, Saffy felt a flicker of excitement.

'*Once, long ago, on a night as cold as death, a babe was born within the castle walls, one who bore the Mark of the Witch.*'

The room gave a slow gasp. Everyone in that kitchen understood the magnitude of what this meant. Children born with markings on their face or differences to their hands and feet, or those who couldn't see or hear were said to bring bad luck. They would be cast out into the forest or sent down the river in reed baskets.

It didn't happen often. But it certainly happened.

'The baby was given to the castle's huntsman, with a swift order to take the child to the forest, bind her to a rock and throw her in the river.'

Arabelle swayed as if she would faint. All the children stared at one another with wide-eyed alarm.

Benjamin put a hand to his mouth and turned to Bow. 'You were asked to drown her?'

Bow carefully rocked his young son and gave a small nod. 'It happened late at night. Luckily the next day all seemed forgotten. But shortly after this I left the castle to become a woodcutter.'

Saffy stared at her father. 'But you took Wild Rose into the forest?'

Bow nodded solemnly.

Ondina shifted in her chair and resumed the tale.

'The huntsman was a man of great compassion and intelligence. He knew the workings of the Silverthorne Forest.'

Verity quietly cleared her throat. 'But wasn't she a witch? This Wild Thorn. Wasn't she dangerous?'

Bow gave a sad smile and shook his head. 'She was just a baby. And her name is Wild Rose.'

'So the huntsman gave the babe a crown of lavender and placed her in the pathway of the wolves, knowing that to survive in the forest she would have to be at one with them. The wolves at once took her into their pack, and it seemed that, even though one mother had abandoned her, a new mother with white fur had claimed her.

'But it would take more than wolves to raise a child. So the huntsman went to the true men and women of the forest, those who tame wolves and mine precious stones and know how to live a full life in the wild woods – the Forest Folk.'

'The Forest Folk? Aren't they wicked?' asked Arabelle in a low voice. 'I've seen the jewels that appear mysteriously in the middle of the night at the castle.

Gems that fill the queen's eyes with sparkle. Surely it's a form of dark magic.'

The Lady Mal laughed softly, almost bitterly. 'That is what the queen would have us believe,' she said. 'Do not trust everything you hear at the castle. The Forest Folk are good people, the same as you and me.'

Benjamin Willows spoke up now. 'I've lived at the Hidden Lake my whole life and never had a problem with any of the Forest Folk. Like the Lady Mal says, they're regular folk, each as different as you or I.'

'So why do they live in the forest?' asked Arabelle uncertainly.

'Because of the folklore that surrounds them,' Bow explained. 'Some people think them magical or dangerous, so they've been cast out of their homes. When the queen discovered them travelling the River Spell, she offered them a cunning deal. That they could make their home within the forest as long as they mined the jewels for her, enhancing Silverthorne Castle's wealth. They could hardly say no. The forest is the safest place if you're an outcast. The queen thought the wolves would imprison them, but the folk were clever and befriended the wolves, so the two now live in harmony.'

There was a moment's silence as the truth of this settled, before the story continued.

'The Forest Folk had great respect for the huntsman's courage, and they agreed to keep watch over the little girl. But they spent many hours in the mines, so the babe was also placed under the watchful eye of the apothecary.'

Saffy stared at the Lady Mal in amazement. 'You know her too? Wild Rose?'

'I do indeed,' said the Lady Mal as if it were the most ordinary thing in the world.

'Where does she live?' Saffy asked, unable to stop her curiosity bubbling up.

'A little with the Forest Folk and a lot with the wolves. All the forest is her home,' said the Lady Mal silkily.

'The huntsman soon left the castle for good. The baby's mother was given a sleeping remedy to make the whole event seem like a dream and the girl, Wild Rose, has lived in the woods all this time, watched over by the wolves and the Forest Folk and the Lady Mal.

'And the only other souls who know of her existence are the people in my cottage on this dark winter eve.' Ondina swept her hawklike eyes across them all. 'And none of you will speak of her other than to pass her off as a fairy tale.'

'I lost the basket of food for Grandma,' Saffy said, suddenly remembering.

The Lady Mal moved round the long oak table and took Saffy's hand. 'I will go to your grandmother's tomorrow, and ensure she and Wilf are safe.'

Saffy looked deeply grateful, but Bow frowned. 'The snow will be treacherous in the Deep Wood by now. Will Lucifer be able to make it through?'

The Lady Mal shrugged lightly. 'But of course. And who says I will take Luce?'

Saffy sat up, a little confused. 'Will you walk through a snowstorm?'

The Lady Mal laughed and tucked one of Saffy's curls behind her ear. 'A forest has many secrets. There are pathways that defy any map.'

CHAPTER SIX

The Warning Bell

In a glade of trembling aspen and alder buckthorn, still rich with dark berries, Wild Rose gazed at herself in a moonlit mirror, a cloak of scarlet about her shoulders.

Most of the wolf pack had run on, to roam and hunt, but three of them remained. There was her faithful Lullaby: a wolf with fur of every colour. A young black wolf with a single gleaming eye. And a wolf as grey as an autumn sky. As she stared at her filthy face in the gilt-edged mirror, the wolves became alert, their ears back, bodies tense like statues. Wild Rose went still, listening to the forest beyond the wind. The snow wasn't as deep here, but still it muffled every sound, making the woods feel spellbound by sleep.

Wild Rose leaned forward, half in curiosity, half in alarm.

Something was coming.

It might have been the beating wings of a scaled dragon. Or the flight of a flame-bright phoenix. (Though Wild Rose was yet to see either, she lived in fierce hope.) But the beating was too low to be something that flew, and soon it became clear it was the hooves of a sure-footed horse.

Wild Rose sprang out of view, swinging through the branches of the sycamore tree with a spectral lightness, even with the drape of heavy red velvet. She crossed into a nearby silver birch and reached a small hanging structure, a nest of bracken and twigs suspended in a cluster of interlocking branches, and wriggled backwards, the cloak folding in round her like a blanket.

There she crouched, peering down as a horse cut from shadows galloped beneath her.

Lucifer.

This was not entirely unusual. The Lady Mal was a keen night traveller, often cantering through the trees without a lantern. What was strange was that the Lady Mal slowed her horse, slid from his back, quickly fed him a rose-red apple and gave a high, haunting whistle.

A summoning.

Wild Rose froze, a mixture of excitement and dread curdling in her stomach. The whistle was a signal to whichever of the Forest Folk were on night watch.

Most of the nearby villagers were aware of the fearsome band of Forest Folk and kept their distance out of fear or respect. But the queen could send the Royal Guard at any moment to make a demand. And there was always the chance of a drunkard stumbling foolishly into the woods to fight one of the Forest

Folk, or a desperate parent wanting a magical cure for their child. The Folk of the Forest, of course, had no magic, but they could offer counsel. So someone always needed to keep watch.

The three wolves prowled round the Lady Mal, and though she stood with an easy confidence, holding out a large sprig of lavender, Lucifer whinnied and shook his head in protest. Wild Rose leaned forward, poised to call the wolves off, when Tobias stepped into the clearing.

In the half-light that wasn't yet dawn, you might at first glance have mistaken him for a stocky youngster. Then you would take in the broadness of his shoulders, his solid posture, the deep-set eyes that peered at you from beneath his black hood. And you might fear for your life.

He had the rough, booming voice of a market stallholder and a thick, bushy, black-blue beard. He loved Wild Rose like his own daughter. And she loved him back just as much.

'Lovely morning for it,' Tobias said darkly, nodding at the Lady Mal. 'What's she done now?' he asked.

Wild Rose blinked, realizing they were talking about her.

'She's been seen,' said the Lady Mal. And the look she fixed Tobias with was so piercing it stopped him still.

There was a beat of silence that felt achingly tense. How could the Lady Mal know about her encounter with the girl called Saffron?

This was not the first time Wild Rose had saved the life of a lost villager. But it was the first time she had told anyone her name. She bit her lip in frustration.

'She's been seen by whom?' Tobias asked.

'Bow's little lass,' the Lady Mal continued. 'Saffron was taking food to Eleena, got lost in the snow and was tracked by the pack.'

Tobias's mouth fell open. 'How on earth . . .?' He pushed his hood back in a state of grim astonishment.

Wild Rose frowned. Who was Bow? And how did Tobias know him? She had thought Tobias hated all the villagers. But now he seemed worried about this girl she had saved, this sweet-faced Saffron.

Wild Rose knew kind Old Eleena who lived with her son by the river. She used to visit them all the time when she was younger, but she hardly went there any more. Not since she'd found the frozen boy at the river's edge. Not since she'd watched through the window as Eleena had held his cold hands, and sung him songs he'd never hear, as he breathed his last breath.

'The girl was wearing red.' The Lady Mal sighed. 'A stunning velvet cloak, or so I'm told.'

Tobias ran a hand through his long hair. 'In the forest? Surely she knew the rule –'

Maybe Saffron has told her friends about me, Wild Rose thought, her heart giving a flutter. She would never admit it to her family, but she secretly longed to make friends of her own.

For her entire childhood, it had been insisted upon that she stay hidden, shrouded by the forest. She had always thought she didn't need protection. She lived and breathed and ran with a wolf pack. But, at the idea that the village might know of her, she found she couldn't quite suppress a shiver of fear. Or was it excitement . . .?

'How many people know of her?' Tobias muttered.

'Too many,' the Lady Mal replied sadly.

'Then we must ring the warning bell. Gather everyone together before rumours spread and it's too late.'

Tobias walked to the edge of the glade where a spider-silk-thin strand of twine hung almost invisibly from the low branches of an alder tree. An autumn conker dangled from the twine. Tobias gave it a sharp tug. At once, a tiny bell rang out through the woods, its chime tuneful and sweet but piercing enough that you could not ignore it.

It was impossible to tell where the chime came from because, in fact, there were many little silver bells hidden in hollows, woven through hedges or planted in tangles of bramble, all linked by the interconnecting twine.

On paws of stealth and mischief came a cloud of moonlit eyes and howling mouths: the wolf pack.

They moved in formation, as if they were part of a dance, and formed a semicircle round the edge of the glade. As they gathered, Wild Rose's six other family members came hurrying into the almost-dawn, rubbing sleep from their tired eyes.

Each wolf found its way to a member of the Forest Folk, and there they stood, heads and hearts level and aligned.

Wild Rose had never seen all her family gather like this before, as if they were readying themselves for battle or about to cast a splendid spell.

Oak, with her short dark hair, amazing knowledge of the forest and her red wolf named for her rare maple-leaf fur: Red.

Jeremiah, the storyteller of the group, a fabulous poet and actor, wise in the subtlest of ways. His grey hair made him handsome in the early light. His silver wolf Wisdom lingered by his side, her sharp intelligence glimmering like an aura.

Akina, who could speak many languages and write with the most beautiful calligraphy. She was the youngest, the sparkiest and the prettiest. Heartless, her huge wolf, crouched proudly beside her, large and black and grey.

Rivern, who hailed from a kingdom of waterways, who could fish in the dark, with no bait and no lantern. His wolf, Evening Star, the silver-grey of starlight, prowled beside him.

Etienne, with his flair for fabric and food. Petite Love, his multicoloured wolf, moved round him tenderly.

Sailor, the father of Akina and the most amazing singer, seeming to know every shanty in the land, stood with Tempest, his mist-coloured wolf, as wild as her name.

And Tobias – or Blackbeard – the protector of the group. With his bright eyes and rugged charm, stood with Rogue, his one-eyed cub the same dark shade as his beard.

Tobias paced among them, muttering about Saffy's rescue and the cloak, the young black wolf prowling savagely at his side.

The Lady Mal stepped forward, long scarves fluttering in the breeze, dark eyes full of secrets.

'She will be known, this wayward daughter of yours,' she said in her lilting accent.

A ripple of unease passed round the circle. Wild Rose gripped the scarlet cloak tightly.

'Half of Silverdel were out looking for Saffy before I found her. It won't be long before news of the rescue spreads and the story of a witch-marked girl who lives with wolves becomes common knowledge. She will be hunted down – and she will be found eventually.'

There was a murmur of disgruntlement.

'How does the cloak look? Is it very beautiful?' asked Etienne, unable to conceal his passionate love of tailoring.

'I imagine so,' the Lady Mal replied with a raised eyebrow. 'But then the only other people in the kingdom who own a velvet garment of this kind are the royals.

There was an alarmed murmuring from round the clearing – Wild Rose strained to listen, but couldn't make out a single voice.

Then Tobias's rage rose above the others. 'Foolish girl. She has to give the wretched cloak back. She can't keep it. She can't!'

'It's too late,' said the Lady Mal simply. 'But consider this. The cloak could save her life, if we use it in the right way.'

'What do you propose?' asked Akina, stepping forward.

She was ten years older than Wild Rose and for a while they had seemed like sisters. But Akina was forced to work in the mine like the rest of the Forest Folk, cooped up in the dusty dark, along with her father, Sailor, and her true love, Rivern.

'Wild Rose must become legendary,' said the Lady Mal with measured directness.

'She is already legendary,' protested Oak, running her hands through her short hair. 'She is the Wolf Child, the white devil who runs through the air. How many more myths must we conjure to protect her?' she demanded, the red wolf at her side giving a swift howl of agreement.

'No more myths,' the Lady Mal agreed. 'Something real. Something utterly believable that makes her a legend of courage and skill.'

The glade fell into a listening hush. Even the bright-eyed wolves were still.

'The Girl in the Scarlet Hood,' said Tobias in a low tone.

'An ordinary girl who got lost in the forest . . .' added Sailor, a man named for his love of the sea.

'And was mauled by the wolves before she bravely befriended them,' whispered Rivern, on a breath of frost.

In the treetop nest, Wild Rose shook her head.

My wolves would never harm me . . .

'I don't like the lie,' said Etienne sadly, running his hands over the beautiful proud-hearted wolf at his side.

'It's better than the alternative,' said Rivern in a voice as soft as the river.

Suddenly it dawned on Wild Rose what the alternative was: *people would believe she truly was a witch.*

It was a frightful thing to be called a witch, and Wild Rose knew the danger of it. She had laughed when Saffy asked her if she was one, but now she felt the unease of it. For even if Saffy thought of her as just a wild girl – if the villagers believed her a witch, the whole existence of her and her family in the forest would be under threat.

'Perhaps we need a song. Something to make her both real and legend,' Sailor suggested.

Jeremiah strode into the centre of the clearing, his stance dignified. He was a little older than the others, his hair silvered by age. 'What we need,' he said, taking in each one of his family and his true love, Etienne, 'is a story.'

And the woods fell silent.

CHAPTER SEVEN

A Legend of Truth and Lies

The story began in the deep, wild forest. A whisper of wonder and wolves and red velvet. A story of winter and a girl in the snow. A story of a child with a fearless heart, who could tame every beast in the forest.

The Girl in the Scarlet Hood.

The story rustled from leaf to frozen leaf, through groves of towering fir trees, copses of frost-glittered beeches and shimmering silver birch. It travelled across the ice-cold river and round the Hidden Lake, winding its way to the very edge of the forest and into the waking dawn.

As the story broke free of the woods, the last stars were fading into a smudge of cloud and the light was the colour of graveyards. Nearly all in the kingdom were still asleep, or so it seemed.

But there are always places where a candle still burns, where the laughter is still merry and horses still quietly whinny to one another. There was one such establishment just along from Hazelmere, known as the Pearl of the River.

Tobias made his way towards it. The Pearl was open from sunrise till moonset, so he wasn't worried about waking anyone. But he wasn't in the mood to be likened to a river goblin or mistaken for a water sprite. His dark hood was pulled up, his freshly sharpened axe concealed.

The Pearl of the River was a tavern perched so close to the riverbank you could lean out of its window and see your rippling reflection gazing back at you. Or simply sail by in a boat, grabbing a quick swig of rum as you went.

This was how Tobias arrived, in a small, unremarkable rowing boat, his oar hardly stirring the river's surface as the current carried him along.

He rapped loudly on the tavern window. Inside, a candle burned low on the sill. A young woman heaved the window open, leaned out and gave Tobias a wonderful smile.

Tobias adjusted his hood and gave her a faint, kind grin. She was only four or five years older than his Rose and already she was the perfect innkeeper, just like her mother and grandmother.

'Morning, Miss Giselle,' Tobias said gruffly.

'Morning, Blackbeard. What'll it be?'

'A hot whisky and a wet rag if you've got one,' Tobias answered in a low voice, letting his hood slip back to reveal a deep gash across his cheek, which looked like a feral claw mark.

A look of concern flashed across Miss Giselle's face before she gave a brisk nod.

'It's nothing much,' Tobias reassured her. 'Just a tussle with a wolf. Luck was on my side, though – the Wolf Whisperer lass saved me.'

Giselle gave a slight frown. 'Which lass?'

'The Wolf Whisperer? The Girl in the Scarlet Hood?'

Giselle shook her head, her eyes widening at the hope of a story.

'Fetch me a drink, and get one for yourself and your ma, and I'll tell you,' said Tobias, placing a bright gold coin in her hand.

Giselle nodded and Tobias cleared his throat as he pulled his hood back up. 'It all began on a winter's morning, at the edge of a forest just like this one,' he said in a voice barely more than a murmur.

Behind Giselle, the straggle of half-jolly, half-sleepy drinkers turned to the tavern window, listening in.

'Once upon a time there was an ordinary girl abandoned in the winter woods, her parents dead or lost or gone. When night fell, the wolves came and it seemed she too would lose her life.

'But the girl was strong and bright and brave. And, even though the wolves maimed her, she refused to show fear. The pack leader, a wolf as white as snow, recognized the girl's courage and brought her into their fold. With the pack, she roamed like a forest sprite and learned how to tame the wolves with a whisper.

'Many moons later, at the edge of our forest, a woodcutter's daughter set out in a scarlet cloak with a forbidden letter. She delivered the letter but was tracked by the wolves. They chased her from the path and closed in with snapping jaws. She might have lost her life, only the Wolf Whisperer saved her.

'The grateful woodcutter's daughter gave up her cloak as thanks and the Wolf Whisperer became known as the Girl in the Scarlet Hood. She still roams the woods to this very day . . . It was the same girl who came to my rescue.'

Tobias had hardly uttered the last words of the tale when two boats set off for the Far Kingdom, the little crew of each boat carrying the story in their hearts. A harpist from Hazelmere galloped off to an inn named the Change of Horses, already composing a ballad about the red-cloaked girl who tamed wolves. And one of the castle guards who'd been up late, drinking, rode the long route home so he could pass by the castle moat and call gently to sweet Molly the washermaid, impressing her with his tale of the Wolf Whisperer, the Girl in the Scarlet Hood.

For to be one of the first to tell a new story is a truly fine privilege. And with each new telling the story changed its shape a little, meandering, stretching, being honed. But it always included Wild Rose and the wolves.

On hearing the tale, young Molly rushed to tell the other washermaids and soon enough the story had spread all around the castle, drifting into the royal chambers where Prince Hugo and the queen's beloved nephew Jonas slept. Lastly it reached the locked tower with its keyless door, where a young girl stood, leaning dangerously out of her small window, her fern-green eyes wide open as she listened, enrapt, to the tale.

By the time Tobias had rowed home, the story had already been woven halfway round the kingdom.

As for Saffy, she may never have heard the story in full had a procession of well-wishers not descended upon her mother's doorstep, offering Saffy gifts and searching out snippets of gossip.

By mid-morning, Ondina had had quite enough of the fuss and sent everyone away unless they needed a cure for something. Salt for a wart. Conkers to stop snoring. Garlic and lemon-balm tonic for a cold. A rich array of gifts had piled up on the table, all for Saffy.

There was a slice of still-warm apple cake sent from Marla. A lovely silk ribbon from Amira the milliner. A peacock feather and a myriad of pressed flowers, small glistening pots of jam and a jar of fresh honeycomb. But Saffy couldn't help feeling that these gifts were not meant for her. Surely Wild Rose should have them; she was the saviour of the story.

Saffy waited until her mother was busy in the kitchen, then she slipped on her blue cloak. But it wasn't quite the blue family cloak. Ondina had stayed up through the night, sipping gin and sewing, so the navy cloak fitted Saffy perfectly, its hem taken up and embroidered in a pattern of silvery symmetrical snowflakes.

Now Saffy filled its pockets with gifts, twined sprigs of lavender through her dancing curls, and crept out of the Ebony House's door.

The snow was ankle-deep as Saffy dashed through the lilac-and-camomile-scented garden, but now the cloak didn't drag on the ground at all, and she moved easily out of the gate and made her way along the edge of the forest until she came to an old oak tree swing.

Here Saffy paused, breathing in the scent of heather and frost. She didn't dare go any further into the forest – her nerves would not allow it – but, even if she'd had the courage, risking Ondina's fury was simply not worth it.

I'll just leave the gifts here, Saffy thought, placing them near the swing. She had no idea if Wild Rose ever came this close to the edge of the woods, but, if she were anywhere nearby, surely the honeyed smell of the apple cake would draw her in.

On a whim, Saffy seized the peacock feather and wrote carefully in the snow, taking time to scribe each letter as her father had shown her.

TO WILD ROSE
THANK YOU FOR SAVING MY LIFE
ALL MY LOVE
SAFFY

She had turned on her heel to head back home when a long shadow moved through the trees. Saffy spun towards it, her heart lurching in her chest, wishing for it to be Wild Rose.

But the shadow was too tall, his face hooded by a dark cloak, a light aloofness to his manner. Saffy shrank back into the trees, trying to keep out of sight, but the shadow moved towards her, bright eyes peering at her curiously from within the hood.

'If you're looking for Wild Rose,' said Jack Willows, leaning against the side of the oak tree and admiring the little pile of gifts by its roots, 'I know her neck of the woods pretty well. I made her a pair of shoes once, to say thank you for saving my brother Joel's life.'

Saffy smiled a little nervously. 'Would you show me?' she asked, her heart aflutter with her fear of the forest and the hope of seeing the wild girl again.

Jack considered this a moment, then nodded casually. 'I've got a few deliveries to make, then I'll call for you on the way home. I can walk you back to this swing before nightfall so you won't get lost,' he said kindly.

'Thank you,' Saffy said breathlessly, blushing a little.

He gave her a nod and stalked off towards Silverdel, carrying three boxes of winter boots.

Saffy gathered up the gifts and hurried home to the Ebony House to linger in the garden, already dreaming up what she might say to her new friend should she be lucky enough to see the wild girl again.

CHAPTER EIGHT

Strangers in the Woods

In her small bracken nest, Wild Rose waited in quiet amazement, bright of heart and keen of ear, listening to the tale her family had woven.

A snow-white lie. Scarlet-cloaked, with sharp teeth and yellow eyes.

She had closed her eyes in surrender, letting the story wash over her like a dream, taking in every heartbeat of her own folklore until the tale came to an end and her family scattered through the forest.

The Lady Mal cantered away on her demon horse, taking supplies to Old Eleena. Most of the Forest Folk headed for the treacherous mine. All apart from Tobias and Rivern, who began shovelling snow, clearing a route to the river. Setting off in boats in separate directions, to spread the tale further.

Once they were gone, Wild Rose whispered her own legend out loud.

An ordinary girl . . . abandoned in the winter woods.

She chewed at her nails, trying to numb the feeling of unease. Was this true? Had she been abandoned? Were her parents still alive? Her forest family never discussed it, preferring to focus on the night the wolves had found her and brought her in from the cold.

My parents died in the snow and the wolves saved me from winter.

That was the story Wild Rose knew by heart. There had never been any mention of abandonment.

'But there are many reasons a child might be left in the woods,' she said to the morning air.

Their family could no longer feed them. Their step-parent did not love them. They had run away, looking for freedom. They were not wanted.

They were not wanted.

She pushed her way out of the nest, suddenly needing to breathe clear air. Peering down, she checked that no one was near. The glade was silent but for the stirring of snow. Wild Rose shot down the silver birch, falling the last little way and landing in a snowdrift, a laugh bursting from her pale lips. She was still getting used to the weight of the cloak.

A gentle howl sang through the dawn and Lullaby blinked her bright eyes from across the glade.

'I'm all right,' sighed Wild Rose, meeting the burning gaze that stared so devotedly at her.

Lullaby eyed the crimson cloak with an air of caution, opening her sleek jaws and giving a little snap.

'I can't give it back now,' Wild Rose said with a chuckle, grinning as she shook the snow from her tangled hair. 'It's part of my story. The Girl in the Scarlet Hood.'

She wriggled in agitation, almost shrugging the cloak off as if it were the story itself. For there was another element of the folklore that hurt her. The real lie.

And, even though the wolves maimed her, she refused to show fear.

None of my wolves would ever hurt me, she thought furiously. *They saved me. They raised me. They love me.*

She sank back deeper into the cloak, trying to make peace with the lie. She understood why it was necessary. She knew the villagers were fearful of her little arm because they thought it meant she was a witch.

Wild Rose had always thought being a witch sounded mysterious and daring – she would secretly have loved to wield magic. But she knew in the core of her bones that most magic was just a result of exceptional skills and a deep, intuitive knowing. To coax buds into bloom even in winter, the way the Lady Mal could. Or to befriend any animal, like her fearless Aunt Oak. The conjuring of wonderful clothes out of forest leaves and thread, as her Uncle Etienne did. Or reading the wind, like her Uncle Sailor.

Things most people didn't understand were labelled as frightening. As witchcraft. That was why the lie in Wild Rose's story was needed. To make it seem as if she'd been born looking the same as any other child, and her little arm was a result of the wolves attacking her. That lie bought her safety.

'I still don't like it,' she said sadly to Lullaby.

The wolf put her head on one side, then gave a long, slow blink of sympathy, and Wild Rose reached out to her, drawing the majestic beast into a hug.

And then a new thought struck her, as fluttery and soft as a baby bird. 'If the story proclaims I'm an ordinary girl, then I *could* leave the forest.' She gasped, the realization touching her like a wish come true. 'As long as I have the cloak!'

At once, the scarlet velvet seemed to wrap itself round her shoulders, embracing her with an elegance that spoke of forbidden ballrooms and moonlight adventures. Drawing her knees up to her chin, Wild Rose could barely feel the snow through the thick velvet.

'Maybe I *am* the Wolf Whisperer after all, Lullaby.'

The wolf did not look impressed. Wild Rose darted a kiss on Lullaby's silvery snout and stood, closing her mind to the agony of the cold as her feet sank deep into the snow. The forest's woodland floor was already ankle-deep in a layer of pristine white. Together, girl and wolf darted in a sprint of joy further into the Deep Wood, the red cloak flying out behind Wild Rose.

If you wanted to live in the Silverthorne Forest you had to outrun the wind. There was no other way to survive. Moving was life; stillness was death. But living was more than just running and breathing. To really live, you had to find bliss in the unrestful dark. You had to charge straight towards adventure with nothing but hope in your heart. And that was how they ran.

Branches bent and parted round them as if to reveal secrets; frosted creepers and stems of ivy seemed to coil back, allowing them to pass with ease. Wild Rose's heart was set on her course and she bounded forward or darted sideways. But her arms and face were raised to the sky, as if reaching towards an even greater liberty – as if she might fly.

So they passed their time in the winter woods running and soaring and laughing. Stopping at a bend in the River Spell to drink the icy freshness. Foraging for the last of the autumn blackberries, which Wild Rose warmed in the pockets of the cloak. Tracking deer here and there, gathering nuts to take home to her family and finding small sticks she might whittle into arrows. As the sun got brighter, the unfamiliar weight of the cloak made Wild Rose stop to gasp. It was hot and her entire body was running with sweat. Lullaby paused, but Wild Rose waved her on with a little shake of her head. The wolf turned and scampered into the snow-white forest.

Wild Rose took a gulp of air and sprang into the open boughs of a wild cherry tree, clambering breathlessly up. She flung the thick velvet off, hanging it by the hood on a gnarled branch, then settled on a wide bough, her feet waving in the cold, swift wind. Then she sensed it.

Something was coming.

She gazed down, wondering if a bear had stumbled too early from its cave. Or a village child had strayed too far from home.

But it was neither. Wild Rose grabbed the cloak, balling it up in her arms, and flattened herself against the broad trunk, melding her body to the wood. She was intrigued to hear voices murmuring softly, almost secretively. A girl and a boy.

'How do you know your way so well?' asked the girl quietly.

'I've grown up on the edge of the forest – like you,' the boy replied coolly.

'I only know the main paths . . . I've never wandered into the Deep Wood, unless it was with my father, and even he wouldn't come on foot.'

'The trick is never to rush. If you're really lost, find a heart tree.'

'A heart tree?' asked the girl.

Wild Rose leaned forward, making sure she wasn't seen. Her eyes opened wide in astonishment when she recognized the boy from the house by the Hidden Lake. And the girl she had saved, who had given her the cloak. They were picking their way through the woods.

What were they doing in the forest? Wild Rose tensed, knowing Lullaby was somewhere close by.

'A heart tree,' the boy continued. 'A base. A familiar point. Like a great tree that you can climb and always find your way back to. My family have a few – we use them as markers. This is one right here.'

And they stopped beneath the wild cherry tree.

In the wintered branches, Wild Rose's heart thrummed in her chest. Surely they would look up and see her . . .

She found herself hoping they would. She took a small breath, readying herself to swing down from the tree and surprise them, but at that moment there came a call, a wolf howl. Lullaby had picked up their scent and was warning her.

Below the tree, Saffy stiffened and Jack glanced anxiously in all directions, both of them drawing sheaves of lavender from their pockets.

'Let's leave the cake and the gifts here and go,' Jack said firmly. 'We can find Wild Rose another day.'

Saffy hesitated. 'If we just keep going a little way . . . I just really want to thank her.'

At the top of the wild cherry tree, Wild Rose blinked in delight. She longed to call out, but the words caught in her throat. She had spent so many years hiding from villagers. So many years being wary. So many years guarding herself and her family against them. It was too much history to be undone in a single heartbeat.

Lullaby's tuneful howl sang through the woods once more. A little closer this time.

'We can leave the presents here. I'm sure she'll find them,' Jack said with kind reassurance.

'I so wanted to know what she thinks of the story "The Girl in the Scarlet Hood",' Saffy said.

Jack shrugged. 'She might not have heard it yet. But she will. The woods are full of folklore.'

'Does she even know the truth about her own story?'

Wild Rose went stiff, her hand clasping the bark of the cherry tree in a fierce grip.

Jack looked at Saffy for a long moment. 'That her mother was a serving girl at the castle who sent her baby to the river? That she only lives because the huntsman saved her? That her mother took a sleeping potion to forget her . . .?' The words hung in the air.

'No,' said Jack darkly. 'I doubt she knows the truth.'

Saffy hung her head, feeling foolish. 'Do you think we should tell her?'

'No,' said Jack at once. 'What good could it ever do? To know you've been abandoned?'

'I know, I know.' Saffy agreed with Jack, but her thoughts kept spilling into the air. 'It's just . . . Wild Rose is so . . . astonishing. She's like no one else. Like a queen. The Queen of the Wild Wood.' There was a slight waver in Saffy's voice. 'I just think she deserves to know the truth.'

'Perhaps she'll find out one day,' said Jack thoughtfully. 'But not from us.'

Saffy nodded as they laid the pile of gifts in the snow at the base of the tree. 'Wild Rose, wherever you are,' she whispered, 'thank you for saving my life. I hope one day we can be friends.'

Then they turned and crept back through the woods side by side, moving slowly so as not to attract any wolves.

In the boughs of the wild cherry tree, Wild Rose was numb with shock. A pain bloomed in her chest as she tried to make sense of the truth.

Her mother had worked at the castle.

Her mother had abandoned her.

The huntsman had saved her.

The wolves and the Forest Folk were her family.

The wolves and the Forest Folk were her family.

'That's why we need the story,' she said determinedly, the tale of the Girl in the Scarlet Hood running through her mind. 'To protect me.' And she shivered, but not from the cold this time.

CHAPTER NINE

The Forest Below

When the moon was at its highest and Wild Rose was sure her family were asleep, she slipped soundlessly out of the den and headed once more for the Spindle Wood. This time she did not take Tobias's axe. Or the horse. She went through the treetops filled with a new sense of purpose. Wolves melted out of the night air to follow her from below, but she paid them little attention. This was something she had to do alone.

I am truly going to leave the forest! No one can stop me.

The thought hung in her mind like a lantern leading her through the woods. She headed to the place where the river ran still and the air felt dense with warning.

I am from the castle, she thought darkly. A place she had always been drawn to, ever since she was little. She hadn't known the truth then: that she'd been born within the castle walls. That her own mother had cast her out. Wished her dead.

'But I'm not dead,' she whispered to the night with a devilish grin.

I will find out who my mother is . . . even if she doesn't remember me. I will know her.

She swung down to the ground, feeling the weight of the 'borrowed' map rolled in her cloak pocket. This time she needed no protection spell. She would protect herself.

In truth, the map was a sketch Oak had made long ago that Wild Rose had found on a corner of the wall in their home, on a parchment etched in charcoal. Oak had lovingly drawn it for her when Wild Rose was much younger, to help her learn the different realms of Silverthorne Forest.

The Wild Wood
The Deep Wood
The Faraway Wood
The Spindle Wood
The treetop pathways
The forest below

It was all there. Every landmark from her life was a scribble on the parchment, every wire strung through the trees, and every maze-like turn and twist of the world beneath the woods. The forest below was drawn in a deeper shade of black. A warning. Keep clear. Up until now she had.

She followed the charcoal paths lightly with her finger and found there was indeed a tunnel that led beneath the Spindle Wood. It seemed from the map that you entered it through a tree trunk near the banks of the River Spell.

Wild Rose took a sharp gasp of breath as she realized she knew the very tree she was searching for. That she had stumbled across it once before, many years ago.

It was a memory she had long tried to forget. The day she'd found the half-frozen boy by the river's edge. Wild Rose had heaved him into her arms and dragged him to Old Eleena's small wooden cottage, but it was all too late.

What had haunted Wild Rose most was the letter the boy clasped in his hands – an inky, tear-stained thing.

> *Our son can't hear sounds. There is no place*
> *for him in the village. Perhaps you can find it*
> *in your heart to raise him.*

The letter had been addressed to Eleena. Eleena's son Wilf rarely spoke and they communicated by making signs and symbols with their hands. The boy's parents must have known this and hoped Eleena would care for their boy too. And yet they had left him in the snow.

'Didn't they know the danger?' Wild Rose almost spat, her old fury rising once more.

Lullaby came to her, wet nose nuzzling the red velvet, and Wild Rose crouched on the ground, biting her lip against the pain of the cold, and the memory.

'He was abandoned . . . just like me,' she murmured.

The wolf licked her face. A lupine kiss.

Wild Rose remembered how she had run from Eleena's on that long-ago day, overcome with despair, straight into the arms of a huge burnt tree. But the tree had done a most unusual thing. It had opened, and she'd tumbled into its dark tunnel and stayed there, weeping, until Lullaby had found her hours later and coaxed her out.

Beneath the cloak, Wild Rose touched her little arm, a bone-deep ache blooming in the deepest depths of her heart.

I was unwanted. Because I am marked.

She shook her head, forcefully shaking the thought away, and stood up. Covering the ache with a truer thought. A brighter truth.

Snow is my mother. The Forest Folk are my family. I am loved.

And, as if Wild Rose had called her name, the white wolf emerged from the trees, followed by the rest of the pack. Wild Rose laughed then, a girl in the woods with pointed teeth and moonshine eyes and a voice as haunting as the river.

'Help me find the fire tree,' she told her wolves.

The moon shifted behind thick clouds and the wolves stilled where the river snaked in a silvery loop, encircling a half-burnt ash tree.

The fire tree.

Its jagged black branches reached out like arms. There was a violence to its posture, like it had fought and lost a battle.

Stepping forward, Wild Rose gave it the slightest push and the bark shuddered, the tree trunk opening before her. Moonlight streamed into its hollow, revealing a tree-root staircase that spiralled down into the depths of the dark beneath the woods.

Wild Rose took a tiny lantern from the cloak's deep pocket and lit it with a flint. She turned to Lullaby and gave her wolf a kiss.

Go.

And the wolf softly retreated.

Wild Rose took a deep, steadying breath and stepped into the tree. The bark doorway rolled closed behind her; the lantern sputtered in the breathless dark, but stayed aflame. Through the woody gloom, a pair of golden eyes in a snow-white face peered at her sternly.

Her heart beat with gladness. Snow had come with her.

'Are you sure?' she asked.

The white wolf blinked at her with such a scornful look that Wild Rose could not help but chuckle. Together they moved in step down the spiral staircase. Into the depths of the earth.

Wild Rose had to stoop so as not to hit her head as the tunnel became smaller and tighter, and they could only travel in single file. Just when Wild Rose began to worry that they should turn back, the ground beneath their feet gave way to dust and they were falling down, down, down, into the heart of the forest beneath.

With a scuffle, Wild Rose landed in a hexagonal clearing. Snow was instantly beside her, somehow still on her feet. Nudging Wild Rose to stand.

The roof here was much higher, and she stood up in relief, noticing that all around her other tunnels led away into darkened places.

It's like a beehive, she thought, inspecting each entrance in the soft glow of the flame while Snow sniffed at each one.

Reaching a tunnel that was tiny and smelled of smoke and diamond dust, Wild Rose stood still. It was a scent she knew well: her family carried it on their clothes and beards. An aroma she had always been wary of, as it marked a foreboding place. It was the smell of the mines.

The next tunnel they came to was an abyss of gloom and nothingness. Its ceiling was high at least, and it felt airy but damp. As Wild Rose lingered by its entrance, drops of drifting moisture touched her skin. It was like being inside a cloud and it made her think of those cold days that came between winter and spring, when the air is wet and the day is made of rain.

'This tunnel leads towards water,' she said excitedly. 'Towards the river . . . or the moat.'

Trying to contain her wild heart, she clasped the lantern and rushed into the tunnel, the white wolf at her heels. A cool draught of air tickled her face and the lantern went out. But it didn't matter – she knew her direction. The call of the river grew stronger, filling Wild Rose with hope as she followed the sound up towards the moon.

The world became damper and darker. Then everything slanted fiercely upwards and Wild Rose found she was crawling up over another staircase made of moss and stone, Snow scrambling beside her, until they found themselves in the heart of a living, breathing cedar tree.

Snow whined in caution, but Wild Rose moved carefully, running her hand and elbow over the inside of the tree's trunk until her little arm came to rest upon a hinge. A laugh of triumph escaped her lips. Wild Rose gripped the wood, feeling the shape of a door. She put her arms, cheek and hand to it. Pressing gently at first, then harder and harder. Suddenly, without warning, the door gave way and they rolled out of the tree on to fresh snow, a ball of scarlet and fur.

Wild Rose did all she could not to shriek with giddy joy. Then she stopped, becoming aware of where she was. Behind her were the twisted thorn bushes of the deadly Spindle Wood, which they had crossed beneath. In front of her was a tall tower, with an open window and the fluttering light of a single candle. Beyond the tower, the rest of the castle gleamed ghostly in the moonlight.

But between Wild Rose and the tower was a churning, whirling moat.

She tilted her head, assessing its current and moonlit depth. It was deep, but perhaps not too deep . . .

In the darkness, Wild Rose smiled. She knelt beside her beautiful, terrifying, snow-white wolf.

'Tonight is just the beginning of our adventures.'

They locked eyes, threw their heads back and howled, silvery, fierce and pure.

PART TWO

THE SECRETS OF
SILVERTHORNE CASTLE

Perhaps all the dragons in our lives are princesses who are only waiting to see us act, just once, with beauty and courage.
Rainer Maria Rilke

The Cursed Princess

At the edge of a fathomless forest, in a castle the colour of starlight, a baby was born at the stroke of midnight.

'She's perfect,' the young mother gasped, her tumbling hair plastered to her brow, her voice as bright as the flames in the fire. Dancing from her chamber, her pale hair flowing behind her.

At the mother's wish, every torch was lit, every door opened wide. Every flag was raised.

The castle awoke to a state of merry wonder. The mother's eyes gleamed as she smiled at her husband, the baby clasped in her arms.

Somewhere a window was open, letting in a snow-laced wind. It skittered through the corridors, full of enchantment.

Three serving girls huddled together. A golden dog barked in the courtyard. The apothecary, who had helped bring the baby into the world, stood statue still.

Near the castle's entrance, a trusted huntsman stood alone, keeping watch over the drawbridge.

Magnificently tall, shoulders as wide as an ancient oak, his skin the colour of ebony. He was surprised when a woman clad in a cloak of deep red stepped forcefully towards him.

'M-my lady,' he stuttered, stooping to bow.

'Tell the kingdom a princess has been born,' said the young queen, her face radiant in the cold, bright dawn.

The huntsman rode away, carrying tidings of the new princess to every surrounding village. Joy spread throughout Silverthorne Kingdom, filling the people's hearts with love for the little babe. For the princess was the most glorious baby. Her eyes were clear as moonlight, her skin rose-petal soft, her hair sunset red.

A great celebration was announced to mark her name and all in the land were invited to attend. But, alas, all was not well.

No sooner had the ceremony begun, all the kingdom fell mysteriously into a dreamless sleep for three long days and three dark nights. When the people awoke, no one could remember what had happened – except for the queen. Pale with fear, she told her tale in a trembling voice.

How just as the princess was named Aurelia, meaning golden, every flame turned to smoke and a towering figure swept into the room. Someone who had not been invited to the celebrations.

A fairy with horns and skin of glimmering green. Her eyes were dark as midwinter, yet strangely entrancing. Upon her back were the huge feathered wings of a raven.

The terrified queen had seized her beautiful daughter, desperate to protect her, but before she had time to flee the wicked fairy had unfurled her wings, sending all in the kingdom to sleep except the poor queen, who could do nothing but tremble as the wicked fairy cursed the little princess.

'Before she comes of age, she shall prick her finger on a spindle and fall into an endless slumber.'

As she recounted the tale, the queen began to weep. The shocked king turned deathly pale. The villagers started to panic. A sense of despair descended.

'There is but one antidote,' the sorrowful queen explained. 'Only a kiss from her true love's lips can wake her from her death-sleep.'

A murmur of hope swirled round the room. The king stood up straighter. And, though the queen was shaking, she looked less afraid.

'All the spindles in the land must be banished and burned!' bellowed the king. 'We will guard her with our lives and, when she comes of age, she shall be betrothed to her true love!'

The villagers cheered. The queen swayed, her blue eyes glassy.

'We'll keep her safe in the old watermill,' she announced. 'We'll make certain no wickedness can reach her.'

And, just like that, it was decided that little Aurelia would remain mostly hidden from the world. The king ordered the Royal Guard to set about burning all the spindles. The queen took Aurelia straight to the tower, where they stayed together – at first.

The villagers were delighted. They had lived through the beginnings of a legend, and they knew they would tell this tale for many moons to come.

As for the wicked fairy, she became a creature of folklore known as Dormevega: the Mistress of Sleep.

Little Aurelia was rarely seen by the villagers except on her birthday, or if a neighbouring king or royal cousin were visiting, then she was allowed into the main castle, protected by her armoured guardswomen. The rest of the time Aurelia remained in her gleaming tower, watching the world go by.

But she was drawn to the forest like a bird to the sky. Its wild boughs and dancing leaves seemed to whisper their way through her window and haunt her every dream.

And on nights when the pearl moon is high in the skies, and the wolves are calling, Aurelia is certain she hears singing.

A voice bright as bone, wild as a wolf. Singing a melody of moonlight and freedom.

CHAPTER TEN

Aurelia's Tower

At the top of a tower the colour of dusk, Aurelia hung from her window. Her long red hair tumbled and danced down the tower walls like a trail of blood. Her fern-green eyes stared into the distance, beyond the deep waters of the castle's moat and into the dense wall of thorn bushes that lined the forest's edge.

The Spindle Wood.

Soft starlight bedazzled the clouds and the sky was a vivid winter pink, making the world feel mythical. Aurelia loved this time of day, but that was not the reason she was leaning precariously out of her window, as if she were trying to drink in the sky.

She was certain she had heard a wolf. It was rare to see one by day. Rare but not impossible. And that was all the hope Aurelia needed.

Show yourself . . . please . . . I know you're out there.

She willed the wolf to appear, a fierce longing tugging at her bones. But the early twilight only thickened, the sun melting away and the moon glimmering its eerie light.

Keeping one eye on the treeline, Aurelia darted away and grabbed a bronze spyglass, before half flinging herself back out of the window.

Maybe it's the Wolf Child and her pack, she thought excitedly.

And then, even though Aurelia was gazing at the forest, her mind was lost to luminous dreams. She saw herself slipping from her window, weightless as a bird, and diving into the moat, the spyglass in one hand, her diamond-hilt sword in the other. She imagined crossing the moat with the ease of a mermaid and rising on the far bank, hardly touched by the cold of the water.

Tucking the spyglass through her belt, in the dream Aurelia swung her sword victoriously round her head, slashing mercilessly at the tangled thorn bushes of the Spindle Wood so it fell back, surrendering to her command. Letting her step through unscathed, until every thorned bramble had parted and she stood in a clearing, a wolf of white majesty prowling before her.

An owl hooted and the dream was broken. Aurelia found herself still in her tower, the spyglass now taking in the vast, star-scattered dark. She set the spyglass sadly upon the windowsill and pushed herself back inside, trying to shake off her disappointment.

She had so wished to see a wolf. Not just because their howls had run through her childhood, but because she needed to understand them.

'If I am going to venture into the forest and change my fate, I must be at one with the wolves.'

Aurelia had no idea how to do this, she simply knew it had to be accomplished. It was the only way to stay alive in Silverthorne Forest.

From the rafters of her circular tower, a huddled family of pink-winged doves eyed her curiously. A finch ruffled its golden feathers, blinked its black eyes and began to quietly sing.

Aurelia ignored them. She did not wish to feel melancholy; she wanted to feel gracious and joyful and all the things a princess was expected to be. Only the sky was so huge and the forest so dark, and the pull of the world beyond her window was so sharp that sometimes it stopped her breath. Other times it made her want to scream.

Her tower, which had once been a watermill, was a large, spacious turret filled with light in the daytime from the two windows on opposite sides. One side looked over the castle's bustling courtyard and the imposing rooftops of Silverthorne Castle. From here, Aurelia could spy many a fabulous carriage arriving or watch departing hunting parties, or see the servants giggling and gossiping when they thought no one was watching. She could see the royal world unfold and feel the emptiness of never being a part of it.

The other window looked over the deadly moat, the Spindle Wood and her beloved forest. From this window, Aurelia watched the seasons change, spotted birds unnamed in any book and saw things that had no explanation other than magic. And it was this that kept her up at night, plotting and planning her escape.

For somewhere, in the dark folds of the forest, she believed there must be a cure for the curse that had been laid upon her – there had to be! – but time was running out.

'I have to find a way to claim my freedom before the night of the Midwinter Ball,' she said to her birds, wishing they could teach her how to fly so she might leave the tower and soar into the forest, high above the wolves.

Because if Aurelia did not escape before the Midwinter Ball, she would be locked in betrothal to a 'love' of her parents' choosing. The ball was in precisely seven days.

Hurling herself across the room, she all but dived beneath her towering bed, into the little dark space that was part treasure trove, part secret den. It was here that Aurelia kept her most cherished possessions:

A small cedar chest containing all the ingredients needed for her spells. People were drowned for witchcraft, and enchantments were frowned upon, but Aurelia had begged the apothecary to teach her anyhow.

When I leave the tower, I'll need these to keep me safe.

A diamond-hilt sword, which had been a secret gift from her guardswoman Ester. Aurelia loved nothing more than feeling its weight in her hands as she fenced round the room, fighting imaginary battles.

When I reach the forest, I'll need this for protection.

An almanac that the apothecary had gifted Aurelia – a much-adored book, which marked the phases of the moon and the turning of the seasons, imbued with potions and remedies and ways to survive every season in the woods.

When I roam through the Silverthorne Forest, this will help me thrive.

And finally a small leaf-bound book of her own making.

Aurelia was done with waiting for princes. She had spent years hoping and searching and wishing to be saved. Yet no one had come. And so she had written her own book of tales. It was every colour of autumn, the pages lined with scribbled stories, written in hand-pressed violet ink and woven together with thin golden thread.

In the low light of the lantern's flame, Aurelia delicately opened the book. Her own story was first – with plenty of space left for the ending, which was most definitely still a work in progress.

She clutched the book to her heart. 'There must be another way to break the curse! There must be . . . I just need to get out of this tower.'

Quickly she closed the book, tucked it away in its little cedarwood chest, and grabbed the almanac and a handful of dried rose petals instead. Scrambling out from under her bed, her endless hair dragged along the uneven flagstone floor, gathering dust, gateau crumbs and strands of half-formed cobwebs. But Aurelia could not have cared less. No one in the kingdom wished to cut Aurelia's hair, for the curse made people wary. A lock of cursed hair might bring terrible luck.

The almanac was old and fluttery like a hymn book, but Aurelia hardly needed to glance at the spell any more, she knew it so well. Setting the book open upon the music stand of her piano, as she did every night, Aurelia fetched three candles, each a different colour. She lit them and arranged them upon her whalebone dresser. Next she seized an eagle-feather quill, her hands quivering with desperate hope as she dipped its point into violet ink. With a racing heart, Aurelia etched her deepest wish across the dried rose petals.

Let me escape my tower and change my fate.

Discarding the quill, she dropped the rose petals into the flames of the candles and watched them burn.

The tower filled with their soft floral smoke and Aurelia sat cross-legged on the floor and closed her eyes, letting herself envision the many ways she had dreamed she might escape. This was not simply a ritual of fire and petals. This was a magic of faith.

For Aurelia did have a plan. Escape plan part one: the rope and the wings.

Aurelia had built wings she felt sure would help her soar from the tower window, over the merciless moat. The rope was her security in case she didn't reach the far bank and slipped into the dark waters. As Aurelia had never learned to swim. So she may also need the rope in case she fell and had to haul herself back up into her tower and try again.

She stood up and ran her eyes over the collection of small winged figurines upon her dressing table. Lifelike clay dolls she had painstakingly sculpted, with elegant, durable wings crafted from real feathers.

She had carefully calculated the weight and ratio of each doll to its wingspan and the power of the wind. Then on calm mornings, before anyone else in the castle was awake, she would fling them from her window and watch them fall gracefully towards the moat.

Mostly they sank or shattered. But over time the winged figurines had begun ever so softly to glide. And if Aurelia's dolls could fly from her tower and soar across the moat, then so could she.

She crossed the room to her wardrobe and reached into its depths. There, among the silk and satin gowns, her fingers brushed the softness of feathers. With a careful tug, the ball gowns parted to reveal a huge pair of wings. They were shaped like those of an angel, but black. Sewn from the long, sleek feathers of ravens, magpies and black swans, they were the most powerful things Aurelia had ever known.

Shoving her hair out of the way, she slipped her arms through the two leather satchel straps she'd used to craft the harness. She turned to face her reflection in the long emerald-edged mirror. Normally she hated her mirror. It had been a gift from a suitor her parents had thankfully disapproved of. Someone Aurelia had never even met.

But with the wings on she felt quite different – no longer simply a girl trapped in a tower, but a girl with wings and a plan. Just another handful of feathers were needed on the bottom corner of the right wing and they would be complete.

Delicately she wiggled out of them and heaped them gently on the floor. With a length of gold thread and a forest pine needle in place of the sewing needle that was forbidden to her, she attached three feathers gifted by one of the ravens that she had tempted to her window with sunflower seeds. Then, carefully, she slid the wings back into the wardrobe, concealed from view, and climbed into bed.

Just a few more feathers . . . She would have to hope that new birds came to visit in the next day or two, or she might have to risk the flight anyway.

✲

Something woke her, and Aurelia shot out of bed, blinking dreams from her mind. The room was in total darkness, every candle's flame stolen by the wind.

A sound reverberated through the room. The low and distinctive growl of a wolf. Not a distant keening call, but a secretive snarl. This wolf was very near.

Aurelia fumbled around for her flint and lit a candle, tiptoeing to the window and peering out. Then she almost dropped the candle. For there, on the far bank of the moat, was a wolf as white as snow and a girl in a scarlet hood. Together they threw their heads back and howled to the moon, and all at once Aurelia's heart was on fire.

CHAPTER ELEVEN

The Castle Beyond the Forest

The very next morning, on the other side of Silverthorne Forest, Saffy had already been up for hours, peering at the bleak, bleary sky. Now she watched in awe from her tiny window as Virtue Silkthread guided a carriage led by two proud, pretty mares towards the Ebony House.

Virtue was Verity's eldest brother. If the villagers thought Jack Willows was handsome, they believed Virtue Silkthread divine. Virtue had been tasked with taking the girls to the castle for the day. It was a chance for Verity to be presented to everyone – including to Jonas, her betrothed, and the queen's nephew – before the Midwinter Ball. Arabelle was there too, riding up front beside her son, a cape of evergreen velvet draped over her shoulders.

Saffy checked her own cloak nervously and pulled the hood up over her dark and wonderful curls. She gave the well-worn toggle a squeeze between her fingers, feeling its reassuring smoothness amid the glint and gleam of the newly embroidered snowflakes.

Then Ondina was beside her, slipping a thin garland of lavender into her hair. 'For protection.'

Saffy blinked at her, confused.

'There are wolves at the castle too. Only these ones wear crowns,' said Ondina darkly. Then she smiled and added, 'And don't let Verity boss you about too much.'

'It's only one day,' Saffy muttered. Verity would begin attending the castle officially once the midwinter festivities were over, and Saffy would go with her, but Saffy tried not to think about that.

Virtue climbed down from his perch at the front and opened the carriage door. The Silkthreads' carriage was perfectly round and crafted from intricate ironwork. Climbing inside, Saffy felt as if she had stepped inside a pearl. The door clicked closed behind her and Saffy sank on to a silk-lined seat. Opposite her, Verity sat in her gorgeous violet cloak, peering sourly out of the window.

The journey was silent. Saffy gazed out too, delighting in the way the frost had transformed the trees into glistening skeletal figures, their branches outstretched like beckoning arms. After a little way, the trees bent closer together, their boughs interlocking and blotting out the sky. A streak of blue glittered fiercely on the periphery of Saffy's vision, snaking through the trees.

The River Spell.

She spotted a distant stag standing motionless as if it were carved from stone. Two glossy magpies took flight from the branch of a leafless tree, in a cascade of snowflakes and feathers. She saw a bear peer through the trees with odd unblinking eyes. *A bear?*

Saffy sat forward, her breath fogging the glass.

It was standing completely upright and appeared to be wrapped in a blanket. As the carriage curled away, following the path off the River Spell, Saffy glimpsed the bear's hands.

Hands?

She drew back from the window, her heart thumping.

A bear with human hands? It couldn't be . . .

'Did you see that?' she asked Verity.

'See what?' Verity huffed.

'A bear with . . .' Saffy's voice trailed into silence.

'No, of course not. Bears hibernate in winter. Even I know that!'

Saffy sat very still and didn't dare say anything further, but she glanced out of the window from time to time, peeking at the fir trees and wondering how many strange creatures roamed among them.

Soon the carriage came up against the Spindle Wood.

Saffy had never seen this part of the forest, but she'd heard about it. A dense thicket of thorns not even a wolf could find its way through. The barrier between the forest and the castle.

Virtue and Arabelle climbed down from their perch and guided the horses by hand round the thorns, following the spiky wickedness until the path led out of the forest, away from the wall of thorns and towards a sweeping driveway and the drawbridge over the treacherous moat.

As they approached, Arabelle waved pleasantly to a surly guard and, moments later, two majestic gates groaned open and the carriage rattled over the drawbridge, then came to a stop in a cobblestone courtyard.

Arabelle whipped open the door and climbed nimbly into the carriage, drawing Verity into a tight embrace.

'This is your moment, my darling. You will meet your prince and learn everything about him. Try to shine –'

Verity interrupted tartly. 'No, Mother. This is your moment.'

Arabelle took a deep, steadying breath. Saffy stared at the carriage floor, not wanting to be caught in the middle of a feud. But Arabelle remained composed, lovingly stroking Verity's cheek and then carefully slipping her daughter's violet hood down to rest on her shoulders.

Saffy's mouth fell open. Verity's coiled locks had been superbly bound into wonderful plaits, each one adorned with little golden gems. The contrast of the gold against Verity's perfect black skin was dazzling.

'You really do look like a princess,' Saffy gushed admiringly.

Verity gave her a small sharp grin.

'Now I have an appointment with the queen to discuss her new hunting cape,' Arabelle explained as they stepped from the carriage into the busy courtyard. 'You will both accompany me. Before luncheon in the Great Hall.'

Saffy tried to copy Verity's poise as they glided over the cobblestones and through a set of steel doors. But everywhere she looked something astonished her. The way the castle walls glimmered like the wings of dragonflies. The way every arch was bedecked with huge jewels. The way the castle was startlingly cold, even though fires roared in every room.

Very lightly, Saffy touched the band of lavender in her hair, rolling a single bud between her fingers.

For protection.

Arabelle stopped in front of a striking silver archway. Round the doors, threads of pewter and iron twisted in an elaborate filigree of thorny vines with wolves prowling through them. She pivoted on her heel and looked the two girls over, adjusted Verity's cloak, then pushed a stray curl out of Saffy's eyes.

'Always be gracious and do not look any of the royals in the eye unless they speak to you.'

Then she knocked three times.

'Enter,' called a voice that seemed to hold the presence of snow.

Arabelle pushed hard on the doors and they slid open, revealing a room adorned with a thousand fabrics, each more marvellous than the first. A room that seemed to be spun from the strands of a rainbow.

'Your Majesty,' Arabelle said with a simper, sinking into a deep curtsy.

'Come in.'

'This is my beloved daughter, Verity, and her assistant, Saffron.'

The queen rose to her feet and turned her attention to them. Saffy felt her breath catch in her throat. The queen had sharply slanted cheeks, blood-red lips, hair like moonlight and skin that had the eerie sheen of marble.

'Verity, how lovely to see you,' said the queen. There was no warmth in her voice. 'What beautiful hair you have.'

She gave a strange smile, more like baring her teeth, and Saffy's stomach lurched.

Her *teeth*.

She pressed her lips together to stop herself gasping.

Those are Arabelle's teeth.

The perfection was jarring. Like a china doll.

Icy blue eyes glittered at Saffy and she blushed and studied the floor, realizing she'd already broken a rule by staring directly at the queen.

The queen gave a high-pitched little laugh, the sound of a frozen lake cracking beneath a skate.

'And who is this little thing?' she asked coolly.

Before Saffy had time to answer, she felt the queen's grip on her chin. 'What pretty eyes you have.'

'Thank you . . . Your Majesty,' Saffy mumbled.

'And lavender? How quaint,' the queen continued, plucking a bud from Saffy's hairband.

'I can take it off,' Saffy began, hoping desperately that she hadn't caused offence. 'I always wear lavender. Ever since I got lost in the forest. It's for protection.'

The queen blinked her blue eyes several times before replying. 'You went into the forest alone? What courage you have.'

On the other side of the room, Arabelle stiffened, her brown eyes wide with warning. Saffy tried to keep the words from flowing out of her like a river. But the queen was making her so nervous. It was like being in a room with a very beautiful, very deadly snake.

'I was going to visit my grandmother. She lives in the forest. On the other side of the Deep Wood.'

'I thought no one lived in Silverthorne Forest but the Fae, who are not to be trusted, and the Forest Folk, who are a wicked, odious lot.'

'And the Girl in the Scarlet Hood, Your Majesty. She saved me from the wolves. When I got lost.'

Arabelle and Verity both stared at Saffy in alarm, willing her to hush, and Saffy wished she could gasp the words back. How could she have let slip that Wild Rose was still alive!

The queen's eyes became glassy and the air seemed to get even colder. 'Impossible,' said the queen crisply. 'No child could survive in the forest.'

Saffy cleared her throat, trying to ignore the crimson flush heating her neck and cheeks. 'Of course, Your Majesty. It's just a silly story I heard.'

The queen did not smile, but she moved her head in a hawklike manner and her eyes gave a tiny flicker of understanding. 'Just like my daughter. She's always bound up in a chaos of fairy tales. Such a waste of time. Do not tell tales about such things again.'

Saffy nodded, trying not to let shame swallow her up.

Three pounding knocks reverberated around the room.

'Enter,' called the queen, sounding irritated.

At once, the doors flew open and three guards scrambled into the room. One had a bleeding cheek; the other held a wet rag to his eye; the third was sweating profusely.

'Forgive me, Your Majesty,' said the breathless, bleeding guard. 'It's the king. A savage bird has escaped in the ballroom.'

'One of those rare tropical ones sent to the Princess Aurelia from a hopeful suitor after her hand in marriage,' piped up the man with the wounded eye. 'Must've cost a small fortune to get it here . . . We tried to shoot it down, but it's taken a liking to the chandeliers.'

'What is your point?' asked the queen coldly.

'Well, King Aspen has . . . been attacked by the creature.'

'You're a brilliant shot, Your Majesty,' the guard said, rambling on. 'With the king injured, we wondered if you could shoot the bird down for us.'

'I could catch it,' said Saffy, astounding even herself.

The room seemed to gasp as one. The queen stared hard at her, then gave a small shrug.

'All right, forest girl,' she sighed in an amused tone. 'Let's see if you can ensnare his awful bird.'

Saffy gathered her blue cloak tightly to her and hurried after the guards, her heart rattling in her chest.

CHAPTER TWELVE

The Blue Bird

The guards were in such a hurry they did not travel by the servants' walkways but instead marched along the royal hallway. Their boots were so loud it drowned out Saffy's own footsteps. They rushed through decadent dining halls, studies full of artefacts, along passageways lined with peculiar stuffed beasts, down a grandiose staircase, across the wind-whipped courtyard and up to the vast doors of the ballroom. Another grey filigree forest gilded this archway, only this time the wolves' eyes had been set with rubies and pearls, so it appeared as if they were staring at you hungrily.

The moment they were inside the ballroom, all thoughts of wolves disappeared. King Aspen stood in a corner, raging with fury, as courtiers and serving maids fussed round him, trying to stop a large gash across his nose from spilling blood upon his fine robes. Two solid oak tables had been overturned, spilling grapes, bread and wine across the star-patterned floor. And flung across the room at the far end was a jewel-encrusted cage of breathtaking workmanship.

All this was alarming enough, but the real source of panic was the noise. A bird was circling the rafters, screeching like a tortured prisoner.

Saffy knew instantly that she would need the energy in the room to calm if she was going to stand any chance of capturing the bird peacefully. Judging by the power of its wingbeats, it was fairly large, but its caw was not like any bird in the forest. The noise was sharp and high and wild. Almost playful.

Is it an eagle? Or maybe an unusual kind of owl, she wondered. But there wasn't time to waste. Saffy made her way to the centre of the ballroom, trying to ignore the fuss.

'I'm Saffron. I'm here to try to catch the bird,' she explained, helping a sobbing maid to her feet and binding a clean handkerchief carefully round the girl's bleeding arm.

'Th-thank you,' the girl stuttered. 'I'm Molly.'

Saffy gave her a kind grin and together they set about turning one of the tables back the right way. The solid oak was incredibly heavy, but together the girls managed to get it upright.

Next Saffy hurried to fetch the cage and set the dazzling thing on the table. She pulled a few buds of lavender from her hair and crushed them into a mauve powder, sprinkling it over the cage and letting its calming aroma seep through the bars.

She felt about in her cloak pocket for sunflower seeds and placed a few just inside the cage. Then, as discreetly as she could, Saffy unfastened her boots, wiggled her feet free and slipped off her cloak. Steeling herself, she climbed a little unsteadily on to the table.

'What in the name of the forest spirits is going on?' came an enraged voice. 'Get that wretched girl off my table!'

'I'm the bird-catcher, Your Majesty. I was sent by Queen Evaline.'

King Aspen looked so incensed it made Saffy think of a wild boar about to charge. 'The *bird-catcher*!'

Saffy thought of her father now, of his unshakable composure. How he could defuse a man's anger by offering – instead of a fight – a contest of song.

If she was going to recapture this beautiful bird, she would need to sing. But the king was glaring at her so fiercely . . . Saffy was not a hugely gifted singer, but she knew the lyrical lilt and rhythm of 'How Swiftly Fly the Fairies'. That would have to do.

Before the king could march any nearer, Saffy sank into a low, graceful curtsy just as Arabelle had curtsied to the queen. Then she began to sing.

'Soft as a dream on a midsummer's night,
When the clocks chime twelve
and the stars are bright,
Turn away from the window,
don't gaze at the moon,

*For your beauty and youth will be
gone all too soon.*

*Beware the sweet Fae, how swiftly they fly.
They'll wrinkle your skin or steal your eye.
They'll blacken your teeth and turn your hair grey.
Then how swiftly they'll fly at first light of day.*

*Soft as a wish on a midsummer's eve,
When you hope and you dream
and dare to believe,
Don't skip to the forest, to the fairies' ring,
Or never again will your sweet voice sing.*

*Beware the sweet Fae, how swiftly they fly.
They'll curdle the milk and sour the rye,
They'll steal all your silver,
swap diamonds for clay.
How swiftly they'll fly at first light of day.*

*Soft as a sigh on a midsummer's morn,
When the darkness is chased away by the dawn,
Don't take your children down to the water,
For never again will you see son or daughter.'*

The room had grown so silent, it seemed as if Saffy's voice were the only thing that existed, and if she ceased singing the universe would fall away.

All the while, she was aware of King Aspen watching her intently, almost bewildered by her nerve. She just needed to keep singing until the bird calmed down. She began to repeat the song, keeping her voice steady, and focusing her gaze up towards it.

As she sang on, a winged shadow moved across the ceiling. Without losing the rhythm, Saffy uncoiled to her full height and held up a sunflower seed in offering. The shadow opened its wings and Saffy's voice trembled ever so slightly. Whatever bird this was, its wingspan was huge.

As the song began nearing its end, something large and blue careened towards her. Saffy locked her arm into position and closed her eyes, and held fast as vast wings beat the air and gigantic claws grappled with her wrist. Keeping her eyes tightly shut, Saffy opened her other palm, so the beak could greedily peck at the seeds.

She expected to feel the pressure lift as the bird shot away, but instead it fought and fidgeted, wrestling to balance its weight, until it momentarily settled on Saffy's elbow, its strong wings brushing her cheek. Cautiously Saffy blinked her brown eyes open, being careful not to stare directly at the bird. Had she not been so close, she would have gasped because the creature upon her arm had surely flown straight out of a myth.

It was the size of a young eagle, but its face was small, its black beak large and rounded, its eyes beady and bright. And the astonishing blue of its feathers was the bright shade of seawater and cloudless skies. A blue so warm it burned.

The bird didn't flinch when Saffy laid a gentle hand on its feathered head. It only cocked its strange face towards her. Saffy felt a smile rise through her. She kept smiling and softly singing as she shuffled one delicate step at a time towards the gilded cage and guided her blue friend in through the ornate golden bars.

Retrieving her arm and closing the door was trickier and she took a panicked peck to the thumb. But, as the ruby-encrusted latch clicked closed, relieved applause filled the air.

'Who are you, bird-catcher?' asked King Aspen.

'I'm Saffron of Silverdel,' she said a little hoarsely. 'Assistant to Verity Sil—'

'Come here,' he ordered.

Saffy climbed down from the table, trying not to wobble. The king's expression was heated but most curious, as if he were trying to work something out.

He circled her once, then snapped his fingers triumphantly. 'Is your father a woodcutter?'

His tone was cold, and his face so serious that Saffy felt her blood chill. She didn't know the exact story, but her father must have left the king's service shortly after he entrusted Wild Rose to the Folk of the Forest. She forced her face into a smile and nodded. The king peered at her stonily and Saffy tried to hide her nerves.

'I knew I recognized that song!' he muttered. 'Best huntsman I ever had.'

He seized the cage so savagely that Saffy's hands flew to her heart, but the blue bird inside only squawked once, then put its head beneath its wing. Saffy sighed – the lavender had worked; the bird was sleeping.

'Take this hideous thing to my daughter, but if it bites her, it'll be put to death!' the king instructed the guards. He turned to Molly. 'You can tell the messenger we do not approve the match! We are not sending our only daughter to live in a distant land. No matter how beautiful or savage its creatures.'

And then he was gone.

Quickly Saffy began to fasten her boots. When she stood, she found two of the guards waiting for her with kind expressions, holding out her cloak. She had no idea if this was because of the bird or because they had known her father, but she was deeply grateful all the same.

As they crossed the frosty courtyard, Saffy's throat felt terribly dry. Remembering a trick of her grandmother's, she opened her lips to try to catch a snowflake, but it only made her thirstier.

'Is there a well close by? I wondered if I could get some water,' she croaked rather timidly.

The guards did not halt their step, but one of them motioned in the direction of the moat.

Saffy murmured her thanks and hurried towards the swirling grey water, trying not to cough. She followed the moat round the edge of the castle walls, gazing at the sullen swans and black-necked geese. It took her a little while to spot the well. It was set back at the edge of a frozen rush bank, in the long shadow of a soaring tower that seemed to rise directly out of the water. At the top of the tower two white shutters had been thrown open.

A cream-coloured dove swooped towards the window and Saffy caught a glimpse of sunset-coloured hair as a hand reached out to welcome the bird. Saffy almost spilled the bucket of water as she stared in sudden amazement. She knew exactly who lived in this isolated tower.

The cursed princess.

CHAPTER THIRTEEN

The Princess in the Tower

Inside the tower, Aurelia stroked the soft wing of the little dove. She was one of the younger ones, born last spring, who flew as if it were her life force. The dove chirruped playfully and took off in a wild loop of the turret.

Oh, to be free. Well, it's not long now, Aurelia thought brightly.

Just a few hours until she was finally allowed out. Her own great winged escape would come later, of course, but today she was simply meeting her cousin's fiancée at some big luncheon. She wouldn't be allowed to mingle with her family or the other royals and she'd be heavily guarded at all times. But that hardly mattered. She would be able to feel the cold kissing her skin, to walk in the winter-white gardens, seeing how many small winter flowers and black feathers she could surreptitiously gather.

A bell chimed, calling in the hour.

I must be ready.

Bunching her mass of hair, Aurelia grabbed a seashell comb, leaned out of her moat-facing window and let the bundled-up locks spill down the side of the tower. It was much easier to brush out the tangles this way.

Someone gasped below her and Aurelia froze with the comb in mid-air.

Glancing down, she saw a girl in a deep blue, snowflake-patterned cloak with a halo of dark curls and autumn-brown skin standing by the well, staring up at her.

Their eyes met.

'You're really . . . real!' cried the girl in the snowflake cloak at last.

'Of course I'm real! I'm not a pixie!' Aurelia shouted back, a little sternly.

'No, no. I-I-I didn't mean . . .' the girl began.

'What's your name?'

'I'm Saffron of Silverdel. Saffy. I'm the bird-catcher.'

Aurelia frowned. 'You capture birds? But why?'

Saffy shook her head. 'Not normally, only today. A bird had escaped in the ballroom. Your father wanted to kill it, but it was too close to the chandeliers so he summoned your mother, but she was busy with her seamstress so she sent me and –'

'Is the bird alive?' cried Aurelia.

Saffy nodded and the princess wilted with relief.

'Tell me about the bird,' Aurelia called, and then a claw of fear scraped its way across her heart and she pressed her hands together to still her nerves. 'Wait! Do you remember if the king said anything about the match? Was it approved?'

'I don't believe it was approved, no,' said Saffy. 'The king wasn't keen on you marrying someone in a faraway land. And the bird had attacked him so –'

Aurelia gave a laugh of surprise, her voice a rush of silvery lightness. 'The bird injured my father?' she whispered to herself, her eyes widening with amusement.

But Saffy's face had grown serious. 'They're bringing the bird to you – the blue bird. But if it harms you, it'll be put to death.'

Aurelia stilled, nodding her understanding. 'Then I shan't let it out of the cage,' she promised. 'Not until it's settled in.'

Saffron beamed up and Aurelia found herself warming to her at once.

'How did you learn about birds? Are your parents farmers?'

'No. I'm a woodcutter's daughter,' Saffy said. 'I live on the edge of Silverthorne Forest.'

At the mention of that, Aurelia felt an ache in her heart. But it was not a bad ache. It was one that said, *Listen to this girl – she knows the forest.*

Leaning even further out of the window, she called down, 'Have you ever seen a wolf?'

Saffy nodded solemnly. 'Many times.'

And Aurelia found her heart beating almost uncontrollably. For here was a girl who knew about wolves – the very creatures she would need to be at one with on the night of her escape.

'When? Where? Tell me everything!' she called, clutching a bundle of her hair in anticipation.

'Mostly when I was younger and I'd take my father his lunch,' Saffy explained. 'And once when I thought I might die . . . but someone saved me, a girl who can tame wolves. A Wolf Whisperer. Wild Rose.'

'A Wolf Whisperer?' Aurelia murmured, a shivery feeling running up her spine as the fairy tale and the memory of the crimson-hooded girl with the white wolf merged. 'Does Wild Rose wear a scarlet cloak?'

Saffy smiled, bright and wonderful. 'She does.' She cupped her hands round her mouth and called up in a voice full of secrets, '*I gave her the cloak.*'

If Aurelia had had her home-made wings upon her back at that very moment, she would have leaped from the window and flown by the strength of her own determination on to the frozen riverbank below. Instead she gripped the sides of the windowsill and gave a shrill bird-like scream.

'You gave her the scarlet cloak?'

'Yes.' Saffy nodded bashfully. 'But only by mistake. You see, I wasn't supposed to be wearing the cloak at all, as it was a gift for delivering a forbidden letter.'

Aurelia's heart almost slipped through her bones and fell with a splash into the moat. 'Tell me.'

And the story spilled from Saffy's lips.

By the end of the telling, both their eyes were sparkling with the soft beginnings of new friendship.

For there is nothing more exciting than living through a legend.

Saffy felt so proud to have shared her story with the legendary princess, and Aurelia felt an immense rush of hope, knowing there was a girl in the world who could tame wolves. A girl who could help her once she reached the forest. A girl she intended to find.

Suddenly a bell rang out, sharp and shockingly loud.

'It means they're lowering the drawbridge to let the guests in for luncheon!' Aurelia cried. 'Will you be attending, Saffron of Silverdel?'

'I hope so,' Saffy called.

'And if I gave you a letter, would you be able to get it to Wild Rose?'

Saffy considered this a moment. 'I could certainly try,' she promised.

Aurelia waved, throwing both her arms out like a star. A bold and daring plan was forming in her heart. She heaved her heavy locks back in through the window and rushed to gather the things she needed.

Her best paper pressed from nettles, her home-made violet ink and her eagle-feather quill. With trembling hands, she began to write as booted footsteps began echoing up the stairs towards her room.

Hurriedly she finished the letter and folded it smoothly into the shape of a swan, which she tucked into her dress.

'Aurelia!' came a voice brimming with enthusiasm.

Quickly Aurelia cleared her desk and pushed her dust-stained feet into a pair of neat little shoes, wrestled her wild hair into a low tangled bun that she tried to hide with a large tiara. Something silky smooth caught in her fingers and Aurelia smiled as she pulled a black freshwater pearl from a tendril of her hair and popped it into the folded swan letter just as the trapdoor in the middle of the room flew open and her three guardswomen – Iris, Evie and Ester – came bursting in.

Evie with her night-dark skin and sparkling eyes, Iris whose complexion was like sun-warmed honey and Ester whose red hair was the same bright shade as Aurelia's. These three women had been more of a family to Aurelia than anyone she was bound to by blood.

Especially Ester, who had given her the diamond-hilt sword and taught her to yield it, often becoming emotional and claiming Aurelia was just like her mother. Even though Aurelia had never seen the queen use a sword.

The guardswomen were dressed in heavy, glistening armour, each with a sheathed sword at their waist. Between them they hauled a huge gold cage adorned with jewels. But none of the jewels could compare with the splendour of the vivid blue bird who peered sleepily from within.

The three armoured women set the cage down upon the whalebone dresser, and Aurelia beamed at the bird lovingly, but refrained from getting too close.

'Come on, it's almost time for the grand banquet!' the guardswomen chorused, fussing round Aurelia.

'This is in honour of Jonas's engagement?' Aurelia asked a little nervously, wanting to make trebly sure she had the facts straight. There were so many cousins to remember and she was allowed out of the tower so rarely that it was hard to recall them all.

'Yes!' said Evie with a laugh, giving Aurelia's cheek an affectionate pinch. 'He's marrying Verity Silkthread of Silverdel.'

Aurelia rolled her eyes. Jonas was after the throne and made no secret of it, doubting that anyone regal would want to marry Aurelia because of the curse.

Fine. Let him have the kingdom, she thought lightly.

Then it was time to leave the tower, descending a stone-cold spiral staircase down and down and down to another world. A kingdom that was often beyond Aurelia's reach. A kingdom that would one day be hers. Or so everyone except Jonas thought . . .

But not if I escape before the Midwinter Ball.

CHAPTER FOURTEEN

The Secret Letter

Halfway down the turret, Evie took a large rusted key from within her chain mail and unlocked a stone door that was carved into the wall and so well hidden it was barely noticeable.

Aurelia took a breath as the door creaked towards her, revealing the little timber bridge suspended in mid-air, which swayed with the tug and pull of winter gusts. This bridge was the only thing that linked her turret to the main castle.

Wind tore at Aurelia's hair, threatening to dislodge her tiara, and she laughed at the wild joy of it.

Then, holding hands, the four women crossed the swaying bridge and entered the castle.

The warmth inside hit Aurelia, overwhelming her. She was used to the airy cool of her tower. The castle corridors felt too heated, like walking through warm fog.

She moved through them in a dreamlike state, Ester and Iris flanking her while Evie strode in front, swords drawn, their heads swivelling so they could assess every angle. The heavy tread of armoured feet echoed off the walls and the castle cleared at the sound of them. Serving folk drew back in alarm, the other guards bowing in respect. All of them nodding to the fearsome women and glancing slyly past them to steal a glimpse of the cursed princess.

Aurelia tried not to let it fluster her, but her visits into her own home were so rare. The press of curious eyes was always so startling, as if to others she were not simply a princess but a star that had slipped from the heavens and become a girl of skin and bone and flame-coloured hair.

Turning a corner and descending a staircase, they were suddenly outside. Aurelia almost cried out in gratitude. To feel the light touch of snowflakes on her skin and the smooth bump of the cobblestones beneath her feet lifted her heart. She took in the nearness of the moat, breathed in the scent of winter camellias and gazed longingly at the open drawbridge and the path that led to the forest.

'Ready, Princess?' asked Iris, giving her a wink as they approached the ballroom.

Aurelia tilted her chin to the skies and gave a brisk nod. The three guardswomen lowered their visors and the ballroom doors swung open.

For a moment, Aurelia was stunned by the sea of faces that turned to stare at her. But rather than keeping her eyes to the ground, as her mother had taught her, she glanced swiftly around the room and smiled at the assembled guests.

Ester lay a gentle hand upon her back, a gesture of deep reassurance.

Aurelia stood as straight as if a small library of books were balanced upon her head and attempted a curtsy to the throne table, wondering if her tiara was still crooked.

The moment she raised her head, the queen was upon her. 'Why is your hair such a bizarre mess?'

Aurelia didn't flinch. 'This is my preferred style, Mother,' she said calmly.

'You look ridiculous,' the queen hissed.

Evie, Iris and Ester stepped closer, swirling protectively round Aurelia.

'We can fix it, Your Majesty, with just a few pins. But it shows off the tiara so nicely,' they chorused smoothly.

The king glanced over, his expression listless, as if Aurelia's presence were nothing but a nuisance to him.

'It'll never do! Take it down,' snapped the queen, pulling so hard at her daughter's hair that Aurelia's neck tensed as her hair cascaded down her back and over the star-tiled floor.

A hush whispered round the room as they all took in the hair. So long, so wild, so fiery.

Aurelia felt her cheeks turn scarlet as her little brother Hugo sniggered. A boy with the same silver hair and river-blue eyes as her mother looked up in amusement. But there was no kindness in his stare. It took Aurelia a beat before she forced a smile at him and Jonas glibly grinned back.

Jonas did not normally reside in Silverthorne Castle, but the queen had brought him here from the mountains last spring. Aurelia remembered the story of how her mother had arranged a match with a girl from the village in exchange for the girl's mother's teeth, or something equally preposterous. And now here he was at the high table, behaving as if the kingdom were his.

'This is my betrothed,' said Jonas, standing as he gestured to the beautiful girl beside him. 'Veronique.'

'Verity,' cooed the girl.

'Forgive me.' Jonas smiled, turning to kiss his fiancée's gloved hand.

The girl – Verity – was so extraordinarily beautiful it quite dazzled Aurelia for a moment.

'It's wonderful to meet you.' Aurelia beamed, trying to focus on her plan: to give the letter to Saffy. 'I am most excited about the Midwinter Ball and can't wait to dance and converse with you then.'

The royals stared at her with looks of mild surprise. They weren't used to her being so animated.

'I would also like to show my gratitude,' Aurelia continued in a rush, 'to the bird-catcher. I owe a debt of gratitude to whoever saved the blue bird's life as it is a most wonderful gift.'

The queen glared at her daughter a little sourly and snapped, 'Well, show yourself, forest girl.'

'It was me. And you are welcome, Princess,' chirruped a low, nervous voice.

Aurelia slipped a swan-shaped letter into Ester's hands, nodding in the bird-catcher's direction.

'A letter of thanks,' she said, dipping her head.

Saffy took the letter graciously and placed it carefully within the folds of her dress.

The queen gave a harried sigh, the guardswomen gripped their swords a little tighter and Aurelia understood the signal. It was time to leave.

Out into the snow-laced day, they went to gather winter camellias and feathers before returning to the solitary tower. And, at every step, Aurelia's heart beat with a swift and wondrous hope.

CHAPTER FIFTEEN

Into the Wild Wood

Twilight twinkled across the restless sky and Saffy stood at the edge of the moat, watching cautiously as two guards lowered the drawbridge and Virtue Silkthread clattered across it in the wrought-iron carriage.

The luncheon had been endlessly long and, by the time it was done, most of the royals seemed drunk and disinterested. Its brightest moment had been the brief visit from the princess.

Jonas had continued to get Verity's name wrong, speak over her and stare hungrily at her beautiful face. Saffy had found him quite intimidating – he carried the same sharp sense of self-importance as the queen.

But Verity had regarded him curiously, and at first Saffy had presumed she was simply very taken with his wonderfully embroidered clothes, and his many silver rings and starry medallions. Yet after a time Saffy realized Verity was studying him. Trying to spot his weaknesses, seeing how she might outsmart him. Her moment finally came when his younger cousin, the little prince Hugo, Aurelia's only brother, had recounted the tale of the Girl in the Scarlet Hood and Verity had coolly proclaimed that the very same red cloak had once been hers.

Saffy had been quite shocked. But Jonas had suddenly paid attention. He didn't get Verity's name wrong after that, but talked endlessly about 'when he was king, he would hunt any wild thing in the woods'. Saffy hoped that day would never come.

As Virtue drew the carriage to a stop, she called to him. 'Would you mind if I sat up front with you? I'm used to travelling in the open air and I do so love the forest.'

Virtue gave a casual shrug, and Verity pulled her mother Arabelle into the carriage, abruptly closing the door on Saffy in agreement.

Climbing up to perch behind the horses, Saffy tried to swallow down her fear. If she was going to deliver the letter to Wild Rose, she would have to be brave.

She straightened up as Virtue called to the horses and the carriage rolled away. The bite of the wind on her face felt lovely after the stagnant air of the castle, and the stars seemed so close that Saffy felt sure she could reach up and catch one. The lantern at the front of the carriage jostled and bounced, casting dancing shadows.

To Saffy's right, the River Spell shone a ghostly silver, snaking its way through the woods. To her left, she caught the scent of smoke. Glancing up, Saffy even glimpsed a thin, smoky line curling its way round the trees. She swivelled abruptly to look over her shoulder and almost fell from her seat with shock.

Two bears, in human clothes, stood back from the pathway in the shelter of a large elm tree. One with a small harp, one with a smoking pipe.

They were only there for a split second, captured in the glow of lanternlight, before the carriage rolled on, and the night rolled in, and it seemed they had never been there at all.

'You all right, Miss Saffy?' asked Virtue.

'Yes,' she said. 'I just thought I smelled smoke.'

'Probably a woodcutter keeping warm,' Virtue said confidently, but a frown deepened across his brow.

Gathering in the reins, he geed the horses into an easy trot and, for a while, the journey was peaceful. Then a different movement caught Saffy's eye. Something blacker than the forest air, solid in its lupine stance, was skulking alongside them. One of the horses reared in alarm; the other began straining to bolt.

Virtue leaped down and seized their bridles to calm them as a young wolf the colour of thunder emerged from a thicket of bushes. When it blinked, Saffy saw that it had only one eye. Virtue swiftly pulled a bow and arrow from beneath the seat and began to take aim.

'Wait!' cried Saffy.

Virtue hesitated for a split second and a voice sang out in lullaby tones.

Virtue lowered the bow and arrow, peering sharply about him. 'The language of the Fae,' he muttered warily.

Saffy glanced round in fierce hope. It was Wild Rose. It had to be. The wolf howled once, then slunk away into the blackness of the night woods. The song ended and Virtue blinked as if he were awakening from a dream.

'What have we stopped for?' came an irritable voice from the carriage window.

'Nothing much, just a wolf,' answered Virtue as he climbed back up and urged the startled horses on.

'Did you see anything?' he asked Saffy in a low voice.

'No. But I'm sure it was Wild Rose.'

'Or Dormevega,' added Virtue fearfully.

Saffy considered dropping the letter to the ground somewhere Wild Rose might see it, but she knew the snow would smudge the violet ink and the message would be lost. She would have to sneak away after Virtue had dropped her home and find her way to the wild cherry tree.

As the carriage rumbled nearer to the edge of Silverthorne Forest, a chestnut horse galloped towards them. Virtue slowed the carriage to a halt and Saffy strained through the darkness to see who it was.

'Jack,' Virtue said. 'Are you making deliveries at night?'

'I was hoping to catch your carriage,' answered Jack Willows calmly.

'Oh,' said Virtue, looking a little grave. 'If it's my sister you're after, she's in the carriage with our mother. We've just come from the castle and –'

'It's about the shoes,' Jack said, interrupting him.

'The shoes?'

'For the Midwinter Ball.'

Jack must have known the shoes had been an excuse for Saffy to run the errand, but he had made them anyway, she realized – touched suddenly by the sadness of his and Verity's ill-fated love. Knowing that Arabelle would never allow such a gift to pass between them, she suddenly had an idea.

'I'm sure Verity will be delighted with them,' said Saffy kindly. 'I'll give her the shoes when we're alone,' she offered, leaning forward to take the parcel from Jack. As she drew in close, she daringly whispered to him.

'Would you leave this letter by the heart tree . . . for Wild Rose?' She handed the folded swan to Jack before he had time to refuse.

Jack nodded, tipped his hat, then turned the horse about and rode away. Neither Saffy nor Jack noticed the opened window of the carriage or Verity's face peering out of it, her eyes following the boy on the horse, quiet tears spilling down her cheeks.

The carriage rolled and bumped out of the woods and Saffy was surprised to find a horse the shade of shadow standing in her garden, chewing on a frosted branch of the pear tree.

The Lady Mal must be here . . .

Gathering her cloak about her and clutching the precious shoes, Sàffy thanked the Silkthreads, hopped down from her perch and ran to the back door, her footsteps muted by the deep snow.

'Already they speak of her at the castle.' Saffy heard the lilting voice of the apothecary over the freezing air.

'What do they say?' asked Saffy's father.

'Only the legend we have created, the Girl in the Scarlet Hood.'

Saffy froze on the threshold of her home, listening hard.

'And what of the queen?' said Ondina.

'The queen does not remember, but I can't say for how long.'

'What about King Aspen?' asked Bow.

'He's none the wiser. His only concern is getting the girl he believes to be the princess married before the curse strikes.'

Saffy shivered. *The girl he believes to be the princess . . .* She ran over the words in her mind, trying to make sense of them. There was only one princess at Silverthorne Castle and certainly only one that was cursed. Aurelia.

'If it wasn't for that wicked curse,' said Ondina sourly. And then, in a gentler tone, she asked, 'How is little Briar . . . stuck in that tower all day?'

'She's restless,' answered the Lady Mal.

Saffy went rigid with confusion. Who was Briar? It was Aurelia who was imprisoned in the tower.

'What stage are the Folk of the Forest at with the Rising? How soon could they be ready?'

'From what I know, they're close,' the Lady Mal replied, 'but I will speak with Tobias to make sure.'

'And Wild Rose?' asked Ondina. 'Does she know of the princess?'

'She knows the folklore, nothing more.'

'You suppose they must both be aware of each other,' said Ondina thoughtfully. 'Just as long as they never meet . . .'

The Lady Mal laughed softly. 'With one in the castle and one in the forest, it's highly unlikely they ever would.'

Saffy's thoughts were whirling as the conversation moved on to talk of tonics and potions. Briar, the Rising, so many things she didn't understand. But there was one thing she was certain of.

Wild Rose will *know of the princess. Just as soon as she reads the letter.*

CHAPTER SIXTEEN

Midnight Destiny

Wild Rose breathed in the scent of the wind, waiting until the little carriage had rolled away. She drew up her crimson hood and tapped Rogue on the nose.

'No more troubling the villagers,' she whispered.

He whined softly and licked her face.

'Go on with you,' she chuckled, letting her cloak fall open, revealing a small lantern looped over the crook of her elbow. Carefully she swung herself up into the bough of a crooked larch tree. The ground was hardening to an icy solidness, like the surface of the Hidden Lake.

Nearly time for winter boots, she thought with a sigh. Etienne made her a pair of rabbit-fur boots every autumn, even though she insisted she didn't need them. But Wild Rose knew that you couldn't argue with ice. Snow she could outrun, but once the ice set in, winter always won. 'But not yet.'

She was miles from the glade, the night was young and her wolves were singing. She joined their moonlit call, her voice raw with the melody of the forest – the burn of the wind and lilt of the river and the deathly nights of winter.

Yellow eyes glowed and blinked as subtle as stars, and Lullaby emerged through a frozen musk patch, her fur carrying its frosty scent. Her sweet howl joining the melody in a chorus of silver.

With the darkening of the nights and the stealthy approach of midwinter, it was time to make the garlands her family hung in the glade each year for her birthday.

Her birthday.

It was normally a happy time, her favourite time, when she gathered long stems of frosted ivy, a sprig of winter cherry blossom and armfuls of thistle to decorate the trees. But this year felt different. The conversation between Saffy and the boy she'd overheard the night before last was still so fresh in her mind.

The truth about her own mother still stung.

The wolves and the Folk of the Forest are my family. Snow is my mother.

A growl arose from Lullaby's throat, full of warning. Heartless and Wisdom slunk from the bracken, the three wolves forming a ring round the larch tree, their hackles rising. Wild Rose lowered herself slowly to the ground.

Someone's here.

She cast about her in the low glow of her lantern, closing her eyes, feeling the crackle and hush of the woods.

There.

Like a kiss blown upon the wind, the sound of a horse breathing.

The wolves moved towards the sound, but Wild Rose hung back, judging whether to leap between her wolves and save whichever poor soul had ridden into the woods, or fly into the branches of a tree to hide.

There by the wild cherry tree was an unfamiliar shadow. A chestnut horse began snorting in agitation, turning its head sharply left and right, startled by the presence of her unseen wolves. Concealing the lantern within the folds of her scarlet cloak, she edged nearer.

Ordinarily Wild Rose did not approach villagers unless they were in terrible danger. Years of warnings from her family were hard to shake.

'People are foolish. They will think you a witch. It's too dangerous,' Jeremiah would tell her softly, before spinning her a wonderful bedtime tale.

Wild Rose had always laughed this notion off. But not any more.

My mother abandoned me because she feared I was a witch.

The icy truth of it made her weary. Weary. But not afraid.

Closer now, she could see that the rider looked young. He slid from the horse's back with ease and seemed to tuck something down at the roots of the wild cherry tree. She realized then that this was the same tree where Saffy and the boy had left the gifts for her. The same boy.

Wild Rose let the lantern spill its light through the woods as she emerged from between the trees. The boy almost dropped his own lantern as he gaped at her and the three golden-eyed wolves. But he did not try to flee.

'They won't hurt you,' she said lightly. 'Not if I'm here. And not if I don't want them to.'

'My name is Jack Willows,' he began in a low voice. 'You saved my brother from the lake two summers over. My family is forever grateful to you.'

Wild Rose nodded. 'You've no need to thank me. There are so many dangers in the woods.'

'That's most noble.'

Her face lit up in a smile, her pointed teeth and ice-blue eyes making her look elven.

Jack had the strangest sensation as he gazed at her. She reminded him of someone . . . Only he did not quite know who.

'I have something for you, Miss Rose,' he explained, retrieving the letter he had placed in the ancient roots of the wild cherry tree.

It was swan-shaped, made of paper, its wings waiting to be unfolded. Cautiously he moved towards her, placing the letter in her outstretched hand.

As she took it, she felt the brush of fur round her ankles. The wolves were getting restless. It was time to move.

'Farewell, Jack Willows,' she called, and then she was gone, into the trees, leading the wolves away. Leaving the boy gazing after her, quite star-struck.

When she was certain she was alone, Wild Rose clambered up and lay across the branches of two overlapping willow trees. Positioning the lantern on an overhanging bough and pulling the cloak tightly round her, she carefully opened the folded swan. Inside was a note addressed just to her and a lovely black freshwater pearl.

Dearest Wild Rose,

I am the princess who lives in the tower of Silverthorne Castle. My name is Aurelia, and I'm cursed.

I am destined to prick my finger on a spindle and fall into a wakeless sleep, which only true love's kiss can save me from. But I cannot wait and hope for true love's kiss.

I know your legend. I know you changed your own fate and tamed the Silverthorne wolves. Oh, what freedom I imagine you must have!

I am due to be betrothed on the night of the Midwinter Ball, but I plan to flee this place and rewrite my destiny. Can you help me learn to tame the wolves? I intend to break the wicked

fairy's curse upon me, and I'll need your help
to survive in the forest after I escape.

Please come by night to the bank of the
castle moat. Call three times, like an owl, and
I'll hear you. I will tell you my plan when I see
you.

Your hopeful friend,
  Aurelia

PS The pearl is a gift from the River Spell. Wear
it as you wish.

Wild Rose was filled with fierce joy. The kind that
sings to your soul and makes your every dream seem
infinitely possible. As if the whole universe and all its
wonders suddenly belonged to her.

Never before had she received a letter addressed
to her. Never before had she been given a gift so
lovely as the freshwater pearl. Never before had a
'hopeful friend'.

Wild Rose stayed in the trees for a long while as
she let the words seep in. Slowly a new thought
occurred to her.

I shall go tonight.

'I'm going to the castle – this time by royal
invitation, Lullaby,' she whispered.

In reply, the wolf gave a low growl of warning.

Wild Rose held up the pearl to the light and found
several strands of red hair knotted round it. It would
make a wonderful necklace. She'd wear it with pride.

CHAPTER SEVENTEEN

The Night Visitor

Something woke Aurelia and she sat up, the swirling nearness of her dream clouding her vision.

Had she dreamed a wolf? Often their keening cries woke her. Blinking sleep from her eyes, she gazed into the dusty rafters where her feathered family ruffled their wings. They were all wide awake. Eyes alert. Bodies poised for flight.

The blue bird perched, regal and focused, inside the gilded cage, wings outstretched, its tropical feathers pushing through the golden bars.

Something had woken the birds. Aurelia held her breath, reaching for the flint to light her bedside candle. She heard a sound again.

Three calls of an owl.

Aurelia shot out of bed and, shielding the candle so its flame would not go out, she opened the shutters and leaned over the windowsill. She knew the guards never bothered with this side of the castle by night.

As long as the drawbridge was raised, the moat and the Spindle Wood were Aurelia's protection. No one ever got through them. Until now.

There in the moonlight on the bank of the moat stood a wolf made of winter and a girl in a scarlet cloak.

Aurelia trembled with hope.

As their eyes met, a beat passed between the two girls. Not the beat of a heart or a wing, but a beat out of time – the space between chimes where two tales cross paths. And, at that moment, two girls out of legend became real.

'Wild Rose.'

'Princess Aurelia.' Wild Rose bowed, deep and majestic. 'Has anyone climbed through your window before?'

Aurelia blinked in alarm. No one had ever entered her tower that way. 'You cannot cross the moat,' she replied. 'It's too dangerous.'

But Wild Rose simply smiled, slipped off her cloak and boots and hid them in a tree hollow. Her hair was the silver of starlight, her clothes so ragged she could have been a bandit. But there was a fierce pride in her every gesture and Aurelia could imagine her slaying a dragon.

Wild Rose knelt before the white wolf, lovingly pressing her forehead to the wolf's snowy brow.

'Stay here. Stay hidden.'

She really is a Wolf Whisperer, Aurelia thought, quite delighted.

Then the wild girl crouched down by the moat and reached her fingers into the water, testing its temperature and current.

Aurelia put her hands to her mouth as Wild Rose secured the bow and sheaf of arrows upon her back and dived into the starless waters.

At first, Aurelia felt too anxious to even move, then she sprang into action, grabbing the rope of hair from between her many mattresses. The same rope she hoped would help her escape. She bound one end round her waist and lowered the other over the windowsill. It trailed against the tower wall by the water's edge.

The moat ebbed and lapped, with whirls that could swiftly pull you under. But within moments Wild Rose emerged at the foot of the tower and, through a combination of grit and hope, made her way up to grab the rope of red hair.

Aurelia set the candle down on her whalebone dresser, then opened her arms to the width of her window and braced herself. As she felt the pull of Wild Rose climbing, Aurelia edged backwards, grinding her teeth until, with a last brisk tug, Wild Rose slid through the window and both girls collapsed on the floor.

'You did it!' Aurelia shrieked, rushing over and reaching out her arms to Wild Rose.

Wild Rose flew to her feet, water dripping from her, the bow raised and an arrow pointed directly at Aurelia's heart.

The princess froze.

'Are we alone?' asked Wild Rose. Aurelia nodded. 'And you told no one I was coming?'

'Not a soul,' Aurelia said solemnly.

Slowly the bow was lowered and Wild Rose looked around in quiet astonishment.

'Do you really live here alone?'

'Yes,' Aurelia answered shyly, as if trying to shield her sadness. 'Well, apart from my birds. And my guardswomen. My mother sometimes comes, but not much. And the Lady Mal —'

'I too know the Lady Mal,' Wild Rose said, wringing her wet hair out.

'You know her . . . But how?'

'She dwells in the forest too.'

'She does? Oh well, I think she's incredible! I love her so much,' Aurelia said eagerly.

'I've known her since I was three. She taught me everything I know about plants and potions,' said Wild Rose, softening as she untangled herself from the long red rope of hair.

Aurelia did the same and together they gathered it up, hanging it near the fireplace to dry.

'Do you really live in the woods with wolves?' Aurelia whispered as she set about lighting the fire.

'I do. With the Folk of the Forest too. They mine your mother's jewels.'

Aurelia frowned.

'The Forest Folk? Aren't they wicked?'

Wild Rose chuckled dryly. 'Not at all. They saved my life. They're my family,' she said proudly. 'It's just the folklore about them that frightens people, so they keep to themselves and carry axes for protection.'

'It must be wonderful,' Aurelia went on quickly. 'Living in a wood full of magic and mysteries and fairies . . .'

'If that's what you believe,' said Wild Rose a little darkly.

'I believe in you,' said Aurelia, suddenly overcome with gratitude. 'I believe you could do anything. You live freely in the forest. You tamed the wolves that maimed you! Oh, will you teach me how to make friends with them? I'll need to know how after I escape.'

Wild Rose was still a long moment, her head cocked, her ice-blue eyes unreadable.

'Can you keep a secret?' she said at last in a low voice.

Aurelia nodded and, as the flames of the fire began to crackle, the two girls sat down in its warmth, opposite each other.

'The stories you've heard of me aren't true,' said Wild Rose softly. 'None of my wolves have ever hurt me. I was born in the castle, long ago, but, when my mother saw I had the Mark of the Witch, she abandoned me in the snow, and my family saved me.'

Aurelia was aghast. 'You were born here in the castle? I thought your parents died in the snow.'

'My true mother is that wolf on the riverbank,' replied Wild Rose firmly.

Aurelia smiled as she took this in. 'I wish my mother was a wolf. At least then I'd have a pack and I'd be free and . . .' She trailed off, clearing her throat.

'But isn't it wonderful to be a princess? To have all this. To have a mother who is queen?'

Aurelia felt herself clam up. What could she possibly say to explain the loneliness of her life? The disregard she felt from her family. The desperation to escape.

'I don't trust my mother,' was all she could manage.

Wild Rose looked horrified. 'You don't trust your own family? That must be . . . I trust mine with my life.'

Aurelia smiled sadly and they fell into silence, taking in the light and warmth of the fire.

'Is that why you want to escape?' asked Wild Rose, moving nearer to the flames, but refusing Aurelia's offer of a clean dress and blankets. 'Have you ever tried to leave the tower before?'

Aurelia laughed bitterly. 'Many times when I was younger. It's easy enough to pick the lock on the trapdoor. But the stairway just leads down and down into lapping water, the only door halfway up is continually locked, too hard to kick down, and, in all these years, no one's ever left the key behind.'

'I can help you escape,' said Wild Rose quite simply. 'I'll bring you the ingredients for protection spells, prosperity, good fortune and secrecy,' she explained. 'To help you with your journey.'

As she spoke, Wild Rose gestured vaguely with her little arm and, in a snap of a glance, Aurelia really noticed it for the first time. It wasn't that she'd not seen it before, but it just hadn't seemed important.

'Then I could help you climb down the rope. It's not that hard.'

Aurelia shook her head sadly. 'I can't swim . . .'

Wild Rose was silent for a moment. 'So do you have another plan?' she asked.

'I'm going to leave my tower the same way the birds do. I'm going to fly.'

'Fly!' exclaimed Wild Rose, looking delighted. 'How?'

Aurelia all but danced across the room, flinging open the doors of the wardrobe and reaching through her silks to her extraordinary wings.

'Close your eyes.'

And, when Aurelia let her look, the wild girl gave a gasp. For Wild Rose felt she was gazing at a feathered Fae.

'I've never been able to practise flying in them, but I know they'll work. I've made all the calculations from experiments with my dolls,' Aurelia explained wildly, gesturing to a row of little figurines.

'So you'll leap from the window and soar across the moat! That's astonishing!'

'Yes.' Aurelia nodded giddily. 'But I'll have the rope of hair for safety,' she added, swirling across the tower in a ruffle of dark feathers. 'So if I don't make it to the far bank, I can climb back up and try again.'

Wild Rose shook her head. 'If you don't reach the far bank, I'll catch you.'

Aurelia gazed at her gratefully.

'Just tell me the night you plan to leave and I'll wait for you by the Spindle Wood.' And Wild Rose smiled so brightly it was as if the room were full of starlight.

It was a yes for freedom. A yes for adventure. A yes for finally changing Aurelia's fate.

'I leave as soon as this wing is complete,' said Aurelia, partly to Wild Rose and partly to the girl in the emerald-edged mirror. But the girl who gazed back at her no longer looked like a princess: she looked like a wicked winged fairy.

Aurelia peeled off the wings and Wild Rose helped her hide them once more between the satins and silks in the wardrobe.

'I have to get it done before my birthday. Otherwise I'll be betrothed to someone I don't love, and forced to stay at the castle forever.'

'When is your birthday?'

'In five days' time.' Aurelia sighed. 'Midwinter's Eve. When they hold the ball.'

'That's the same day as mine!' cried Wild Rose.

Aurelia gasped. 'So we were both born here. In the castle. On the same night . . . We would have been friends . . . but we were separated. But now we've found each other again. It truly is like magic.'

She paused, noticing a sadness in Wild Rose's smile. 'Let's cast a friendship spell so we may never be separated again.'

Wild Rose's eyes shone in agreement.

As the moon drifted towards its rest and the clouds began to softly lighten, the two girls stood at the tower window and held hands.

It was the first time either of them had held hands with another child.

Aurelia dipped a stem of lilac twined with hazelwood into a little pot of crushed nutmeg, Wild Rose held up a flame to burn it and they let the ash catch on the wind and be whisked away towards the forest, both quietly intoning the words.

> 'By bud and mist and light of star,
> Our friendship will reach wide and far.
> By light of day or dark of night,
> Our friendship will be true and bright.'

'You should go soon,' said Aurelia suddenly. 'In case the morning guards see you.'

Wild Rose nodded and gathered up her bow and sheaf of arrows, while Aurelia started fastening the rope round her waist.

'I'll see you soon?' Aurelia said shyly, desperately wanting to hug her new friend, but holding back.

'I swear we will get you out before midnight on our birthday,' said Wild Rose with such startling earnestness it made Aurelia want to weep.

'Thank you,' she murmured.

Then Wild Rose was gone and Aurelia was left gazing after her, trying to ease the yearning ache in her bones for freedom.

CHAPTER EIGHTEEN

The Steal-away

The morning was fine and clear. No new snow had fallen and the cold had hardened the ground to ice. Magpies sang through the cool, bright air, their feathers iridescent in the winter sunrise, and a girl with beautiful black skin and glittering golden braids crept from her bedroom.

When they were younger, it had seemed so simple. Verity was the beauty of Silverdel; Jack was easily the most handsome boy in any of the neighbouring villages – it was inevitable that they would marry when they grew up. But now . . . she was betrothed and Jack was losing interest. The shoes he'd made her were truly magnificent – to an untrained eye. But Verity wasn't convinced they were his best work. She'd expect something far more wondrous as a wedding gift.

The only solution Verity could see was for them to elope. They could ride to the Far Kingdom and be married by sunset. Her family would be outraged, but what could they do? Once the papers were signed and the ring upon her finger, they would have to accept it.

A horse whinnied lightly in the frosty dawn. Verity breathed out a stream of dragon's breath, lifted her mother's moss-green cloak and the hem of her skirts in her fists and ran as lightly as she could across the fields, trying not to sink into the snow.

She reached the barn at the back of the Change of Horses inn and was relieved to find it empty of people but full of mares. Five pairs of wise eyes blinked at her and Verity smiled at each horse in turn. She needed one that was strong in body and in soul. A horse that wouldn't quail at the sight of a wolf. A steed that would ride into battle should she demand it.

Producing a bright red apple from the leather purse at her waist, she held it out like a gift. Every horse eyed it eagerly and three of them trotted over, nostrils flaring. But one horse neighed at Verity insistently. She was dappled grey and white, and quite unapologetic about snaffling the entire apple before the other two had even reached it. Verity grinned.

Taking a gold coin from her purse, Verity dropped it in the small jar that hung on a piece of weathered rope from the gatepost, then slipped through the gate, took hold of the horse's harness and swung herself easily on to its smooth grey back.

This was not how you were supposed to borrow a horse. You were meant to clear it with Old Rumi first. Sign your name with a quill or declare it. Borrow a saddle if needed. Then leave the money. But Verity Silkthread didn't have time for rules.

With a swift tap of her heels, they were off, galloping across the fields. Beneath her hood, Verity's eyes held her intent. She stared straight ahead at Silverthorne Forest.

Verity had never entered from the eastern side before, never taken this path to the Wild Wood. But there wasn't time to ride through Silverdel, and she couldn't risk her parents spotting her.

As the horse slowed to a trot down a wide track, an eagle circled overhead and Verity felt touched by the soft spell of the morning. A little further on, a stag raised its antlers to her and she couldn't help but smile. But there was no time to be enchanted; she clicked her tongue and geed the horse into a gallop once more.

As they flew through the soaring evergreens, the filly with her speckled grey coat seemed to merge with the smoky woodland mist and Verity was all but invisible among the trees.

She felt certain she would find the house by the Hidden Lake, as if her heart were the needle of a compass and the Willows' house her north. By horseback, she was sure the journey wouldn't take long. She would meet Jack on his way to the shop, tell him her plan and they would ride off to the Far Kingdom without a backward glance.

But the track Verity was on seemed to lead nowhere.

'This way,' she coaxed, directing the horse into the trees.

There was no pathway as such for them to follow and the horse had to pick her way over unseen roots and snowbanks. All the while the trees became denser. Something white glimmered to her left and the horse gave a shocked leap, almost throwing Verity from her back.

'Stop!' she said firmly, tightening the reins. The horse reacted like a frightened rabbit and Verity realized that she was, in fact, still very young.

Too young to be trusted, thought Verity crossly, but she whispered soothingly to the little filly and gradually they pushed on. Quite by chance, they emerged back on to a track. It was twisty and crooked, winding its way in and round dead or fallen trees.

There was another flash of white. For one bewitching heartbeat, Verity's eyes fell upon a creature that was surely crafted from dreams. A wolf the colour of snow, with moon-bright eyes.

The horse bolted and it was all Verity could do not to scream. They tore off the track and up a steep bank in a panicked gallop, plunging through an overgrown thicket. Branches ripped at her clothes. The moss-green cloak was pulled savagely from her, her scarf snatched away. Verity bit her lip and flattened herself against the horse, clinging to its neck and furiously refusing to fall.

After an eternity of dashing through woodland hell, the little filly finally slowed. Verity sat up and spat in the snow. She felt as if her very bones had been shaken.

'You foolish little beast!' she hissed. But the horse just pranced around quite innocently.

Checking she still had her bow and arrows, Verity jumped gratefully down and stalked away towards a large open clearing.

'Run along home,' she called over her shoulder.

She didn't need the horse anyway, she thought. Not if it was going to ruin everything. Jack had his own horse – they would simply ride together. Verity was certain she could find her way to the Willows' house on foot.

She bound her hair up into a marvellous bun, preparing to walk on, and took a long, deep breath. Then she froze. What was that wonderful smell? It was floral and light, but not too sweet, and it was warming the day, the way freshly baked bread does. Verity turned into the scent, completely surrendering herself.

In her haste to leave before dawn, she had not eaten breakfast, and the thought of warm food was like magic. Dreamily she followed the enticing aroma in and out of silver birch trees, under an archway of holly bushes until she came to a tunnel of hawthorn.

Verity hesitated. The tunnel seemed dark and secluded. Cautiously she tiptoed down it, following the scent like a bee to a tulip. At the very end, to her amazement, Verity found a neat little garden from which someone had carefully cleared the snow.

A garden in the middle of the forest?

She peered around, wondering if, in fact, the garden belonged to Saffy's grandmother. But at the end of the garden was a distressed and deserted cottage. Half its thatched roof was burned to cinders and its door hung open. But, as Verity gazed at it, she noticed a tiny candle flickering in one of the windows. So someone did live here after all. How odd.

She crept nearer. She knew of no one else who lived in the forest but the Willows. And that mysterious woman with her demon horse.

And Wild Rose.

She tutted bitterly. Well, fine then.

If this is where the witch girl lives, then let me see it. I bet it's a hovel anyway, she thought, flouncing towards the cottage and knocking boldly on the warped door.

The sound of the knock gave the littlest echo, but no reply came from within.

The rich scent of flowers and cream tugged at Verity's heart like gingerbread to a lost child. She steeled herself and stepped inside, her braided hair glinting gold in the winter sun.

CHAPTER NINETEEN

A Cottage for Beasts

A dense darkness surrounded Verity and she flinched, but the heady scent of syrup and cinnamon was so comforting it made her nostrils prickle, and her mouth water in anticipation.

As the gloom thinned, Verity found she was in a cramped little kitchen. A quaint china teapot steamed near a blackened stove, giving off the aroma of mint. An ember sparkled in the fireplace. Upon a small makeshift table, three very full bowls of porridge filled the room with steam.

Verity almost wilted with joy. She was so terribly hungry. 'A tiny mouthful won't hurt – and anyway there's no one here,' she said to the empty room.

She was at the table in two strides, settling herself upon a carved wooden stool. Raising the oak spoon to her mouth, feeling the steam on her cheeks, nearly burning her lips with the heat.

'Ow!' she squealed, dropping the spoon and gasping cold air into her mouth. 'It's bitter!' she croaked, tasting marmalade rind, dried thistle and yellow cherries soaked in brandy.

She flounced on to the next stool, desperate to clear the taste. This porridge was pinker in colour, decorated with fresh pieces of rhubarb, a dash of ginger and a dollop of glistening apricot jam. It smelled like an autumn fête, full of nourishment and splendour. Verity lifted the birch spoon to her lips and very carefully tasted the tiniest drop. At first, it was gloriously sweet, then it overwhelmed her with an intense sugariness.

'This is too sweet,' she moaned, dropping the spoon in frustration, hardly caring as it clattered to the floor.

Scrambling on to the third stool, which was ridiculously small, she peered at the bowl before her: a work of floristry.

The porridge was a soft shade of violet and sprinkled with dried lavender, the pressed petals of forget-me-nots and fragrant mauve pansies. It was the loveliest thing Verity had seen in all Silverthorne Forest. And it held the scent of springtime.

Closing her eyes, she lifted a blossom-wood spoon to her lips and tested the littlest bite. It was a dream of sunshine and hope. Verity sighed with contentment and took another little nibble. The ordeal of the morning had worn her patience thin, but the porridge felt like a tonic for her soul. She shoved the spoon into her mouth, faster and faster, until it scraped against the bottom of the bowl.

Verity went quite still; she really hadn't meant to do that . . .

She put her hands to her mouth in alarm, staring at the empty bowl. Someone clearly lived here, and whoever they were would soon be home. She swivelled nervously to glance at the open door. The little stool creaked in protest. Then there was an almighty splintering sound as it shattered into a thousand pieces, and Verity hit the floor.

'OUCH!' she bellowed as her bow was knocked from her shoulder, the quiver spilling arrows across the stone floor.

Scrabbling around the little kitchen, trying to gather up the arrows in the dusty dimness, Verity began to feel tired. As she stood, dusty and exhausted, she noticed another door at the back of the kitchen, which was half open. Through it Verity spied a room full of sunlight and floating feathers, and three gorgeously soft-looking beds. She was transfixed.

She wandered into the room and scarcely thought twice before sinking on to the grandest bed. It was comfortable at first, but its cowhide throw was prickly against her skin.

With an effortful sigh, she got up and flopped back down on to the next bed, landing on a feathery heaven. But the pillow was scented with primrose and peaches. Verity hated peaches.

Slumping on to the last little bed, she found herself in the perfect place for dreaming and her eyelids could no longer resist. Her bow and arrows slid to the floor and she fell into a sun-kissed slumber.

Outside the ramshackle cottage, clouds skittered across the wintry sky and a glacial wind made the trees sway and groan.

A vivid blue bird perched upon the cottage's burnt roof, its clawed feet darkening in the age-old ash.

A wolf dark as death, with a single blinking eye, followed the scent of cherries in brandy up to the cottage's open door, paused for a moment, then prowled away.

A woman on a black horse went by, glanced at the single burning candle and rode on.

Inside the cottage, Verity dreamed of weddings and wolves, unaware of the wicked ways of the woods. She didn't see the three figures move through the trees, then edge their way down the tunnel of hawthorn, through the snow-cleared garden and into the darkened kitchen.

They stopped at the threshold of their home, taking in the wide-open door, the gobbled porridge and the broken stool. The littlest figure gave an angry gasp. The middle-sized one tutted crossly. And the largest one reached for the dagger at his waist.

The creak of a footstep woke Verity. For a moment, she couldn't place where she was. The scorched ceiling. The apple-blossom candle. The smell of dry leaves and the closeness of the woods. A small, furry figure entered the room.

Verity went completely rigid, not understanding what she was seeing.

'What are you doing in my bed?' cried the little figure, sounding oddly delighted.

Verity sat bolt upright as a nightmare unfolded in front of her. A small bear, in clothes, was staring at her, its eyes unblinking. Panic clouded her mind and a scream that could shatter glass broke from Verity's lips as she leaped into the air, charging towards the door, anxiety pulsing through her.

Crashing into the kitchen, she found two more fully grown bears.

'Wait! Come back!' called the smallest bear, chasing after her, reaching out to Verity with childlike hands.

Verity shrieked, clambering over the table to get away from them. The largest bear swore in shock and Verity fled from the cottage, tears flying down her cheeks.

Bear heads. Human voices. Human hands.

Wicked Fae magic!

She bolted with fright, screams burning her throat, and tore through the woods.

What if the porridge was bewitched? she thought pitifully, and vomited into the roots of a dying elm tree.

Something squawked above her and Verity froze as an unworldly bright blue bird descended from the topmost branch of the elm tree. This was it – the madness of the forest was going to take her. Next she would see a dragon. She dropped to her knees, wailing in fury and terror, pulling her golden plaits round her like a cape.

And that was when she saw the wolf.

Her tears ceased at once and she became alert, slowly reaching for her bow as the true horror of the situation dawned upon her.

'No,' she said under her breath 'No. No. No.' For the bow and arrows were still on the cottage floor.

Verity rose as slowly as she could manage and began stumbling backwards, trying desperately to remember everything she knew about wolves.

Don't anger them. Don't engage with them. Don't let them see your fear.

But she was already sweating and gasping with fright.

The one-eyed wolf seemed young and energetic, still a pup in many ways. He began bounding towards her, jaw hanging open. Verity scrabbled for the knife in her bag. It was one her mother used to peel potatoes. But if she threw it hard enough maybe she could at least wound the beast.

Edging backwards, she held the knife out in front of her. Where should she strike it? Its throat? Its heart? Its eye?

A second melancholy howl rang out and Verity's blood turned cold. She knew what that meant. The pack was being summoned.

'Help!' she heard herself cry as she began moving again more hurriedly, the wolf tracking her closely. 'Help! Help me . . .' She was truly sobbing now.

The beating hooves of a horse reached her ears and Verity spun round, desperately searching for the rider. Then, to her bewilderment, the very horse she had been riding just hours earlier burst through the undergrowth, its young rider draped in a scarlet cloak.

'Wild Rose,' Verity uttered.

How did she happen to be here? Was it magic? And what was she doing astride the little grey horse?

Verity didn't care. Relief coursed through her as she leaned against an ash tree, struggling to breathe.

'You know my name,' Wild Rose said, sounding pleased.

The one-eyed wolf sprang from somewhere unseen, catching Verity's skirts in its teeth and giving a guttural growl as it closed its jaws, roguishly, round her ankle.

Verity dropped her knife and whimpered.

In a movement fluid as water, Wild Rose leaped down. 'Don't you dare, Rogue!'

The wolf opened its mouth and howled as Wild Rose wrestled him away from Verity, seeming not to notice when he clawed at her skin or put his teeth tenderly round her little arm.

A single speck of blood glistened on Verity's ankle, but she was otherwise unharmed. She quivered, unable to take her eyes from Wild Rose . . .

Like a beautiful, deadly snake that might strike you at any moment, Verity thought, backing away from her.

The horse whinnied at the sight of the wolf, but Wild Rose caught her reins and murmured something gentle in her ear, and to Verity's amazement the little filly calmed.

'Please, I need to get home,' Verity heard herself beg.

'Where is home?' asked Wild Rose.

'Silverdel,' Verity managed to say. 'I am Verity Silkthread of Silverdel.'

The wild girl pushed her hood back and Verity was able to see her more clearly. Her eyes had the same haunting stare as a wolf.

This girl really is a witch, Verity decided.

'I was on my way to visit a friend and I took the wrong path, and then I stumbled upon a cottage full of beasts.'

Wild Rose frowned as Verity trembled, the words gushing out before she could stop them.

'They were bears, but they had human bodies. Real hands. Bear heads. How can anyone live in these woods! It's so full of wicked things.' Verity burst into a flood of self-pitying tears.

'Come on, I'll take you home.' Wild Rose swung herself up, then pulled Verity on to the horse behind her.

As they rode through the forest, Verity wept. Her fabulous plan hadn't worked. She had witnessed a living, breathing nightmare. A garish folk tale come true. And she had very nearly been maimed by a wolf. She shivered with shame and a longing for home.

No boy is worth all this, she thought fretfully. *I will never set foot in this forest alone again.*

And she saw all too clearly how her life with Jack might be. How she would have to live in the house by the Hidden Lake, on the brink of the forest, where wicked wolves and bear children could wander into her home. How the wind would taunt her. How the twisted magic of the woods would colour her dreams.

Verity Silkthread knew in that instant, as clearly as she knew she was the most beautiful girl in all of Silverdel, that she wanted nothing more to do with Jack Willows. Next time she ventured into these trees, it would be as a princess with a Royal Guard.

The mist-coloured mare broke the treeline with a leap that made Verity's jaw clatter.

'Thank you. Thank you so much, Wild Rose,' she called, springing from the horse's back and running towards the Ebony House. It wasn't until she was on the path to Silverdel that she paused to cast a quick glance back.

Wild Rose sat splendidly upon the little grey horse, draped in red velvet. Ethereal mist swirled round the horse's hooves, making them both seem like something out of a legend.

That cloak looks better on her than any of us . . . She looks regal, thought Verity resignedly and she gave a single grateful wave. Wild Rose smiled, waving back, as she turned the horse round and galloped away. And Verity spun and ran towards her home, her family and her future at the castle.

CHAPTER TWENTY

Twisted Truths

eep in the Wild Wood, the grey horse cantered gleefully through the swaying trees. A north wind sang in the high branches, scattering snow upon the horse and rider. Wild Rose laughed brightly and threw her head back, letting the fat white flakes drift over her cheeks.

Had it been chance or luck that the whinny of the little grey horse had reached her ears through the window of her family's home while she'd been letting the fire dry her hair? Whichever it was, she now had a horse of her own.

And, after the encounter with Verity, Wild Rose's mind was full with thoughts of the bear family. She tied the horse loosely to a fir tree, planted a light kiss upon its smoke-coloured nose and tiptoed along the tunnel into the forbidden garden, her hood pulled up over her face.

The cottage looked even more desolate since the last time she had seen it. The roof had fallen further beneath the weight of snow and the windows were smudged black with soot. The warped door hung even more crookedly on its hinges. But Wild Rose did not go through the door; she climbed into a large magnolia tree and peered in.

Two figures, half bear, half human, sat at a makeshift table, a little girl squashed on their laps. The child was perfectly human, and perfectly grumpy.

It's been so long, thought Wild Rose, remembering the first time she'd strayed into their cottage, when Lullaby was only a pup. The two of them had been out one summer evening and Lullaby had heard a baby crying and, daringly, they'd entered the cottage. Wild Rose had thought she was in a dream world as the mama bear sternly shooed them away.

A few springs later, taking shelter from a rainstorm, Wild Rose had been drawn to the cottage by the aroma of lavender porridge. The moment she heard the bear family returning, she squeezed out of the bedroom window and into the branches of the blossoming magnolia tree, hiding herself among the budding pink flowers.

From then on, all that spring and summer, Wild Rose had made it her mission to spy on the bear family, watching as they set out for their morning walk. She would hide up high or squat down low among the nettles and dandelions, learning where the bears wandered, how they avoided all the villagers, how the three of them always held hands.

One stiflingly hot summer's morning, when the day was humid before it had even begun, the littlest bear impulsively tore her bear head off and bounded into the river. At first, her parents had rushed to stop her. But when they saw how happy she was, how gentle the current was, they had taken off their own disguises and done the same.

Wild Rose had felt cheated at first. Then she'd giggled at her own silliness; she'd so wanted to believe they were bears. The little girl had looked up and seen her. Wild Rose had quickly put a finger to her lips, and that was how their friendship began.

The two girls hadn't spent much time together. It was a kinship of winks, signals and secret waves. And, in a world of dark trees and many cold winters, that can mean everything.

Wild Rose cocked her head and listened hard.

'I can make you a new stool,' said the father, easing off his bear headdress.

'I don't even care about the stool!' growled the little girl. 'Why did you frighten the golden girl away?' She wriggled free of her parents' grasp and started stomping round the kitchen.

'She ate all your porridge,' replied the mother patiently.

'She could have stayed for tea. She could have told us stories. She could have taught me how to use a bow and arrow,' the child insisted.

'I can teach you that,' said the mother smoothly as she pushed her bear head back to reveal her gentle face, puffy with emotion.

'I don't want you to!' snapped the child. 'I want to be friends with a real girl. Why don't you ever let anyone come here?'

'It's complicated, Hester,' the father began gravely.

'It's all because of my stupid sister, isn't it?' cried Hester. 'Just because she got stolen by bandits and thieves, it doesn't mean I will!'

'That's quite enough,' said the mother. 'You can go to the bedroom until you're ready to apologize.'

'No,' said the little girl, folding her arms across her chest and refusing to move.

The bear family had another daughter? One who was stolen from them?

Wild Rose suddenly had a clearer understanding of the family. The bear disguise. The parents' protectiveness of their little daughter. Their lack of trust.

The father ran his hands through his hair, which was the same flame-red as his daughter's. With a weary sigh, he stood and moved slowly to the steaming kettle, filling three wooden cups, before sitting back down and rubbing his brow.

'It won't be like this forever, Hester. That I can promise you,' he said, his voice edged with sadness. 'Once your sister is safe, it'll be different.'

Hester huffed and rolled her eyes. 'You don't even know where she is!'

The father gave a weary sigh. 'Yes. Actually we do.'

'You do?' Hester gasped. 'Well, where is she? Why can't we just take her back? Wild Rose has wolves – I bet she would help us.'

From outside, beyond the window, it was only Wild Rose who noticed both parents tense at the mention of her name.

'Your sister is under a curse,' said the mother softly, her voice straining with emotion. 'We couldn't just steal her back without knowing how to break it.'

'Have you asked the Lady Mal? I bet she knows all about curses,' piped up Hester.

'We've tried,' explained her father.

'Well, what sort of curse is it?'

'Your sister Briar is destined to prick her finger on a spindle and fall asleep forever, and only true love's kiss will awaken her.'

'What a strange curse,' said Hester, looking bewildered.

Wild Rose gripped the branches of the magnolia tree to stop herself falling.

Cursed to prick her finger. Only true love's kiss will awaken her.

There was only one person in all the kingdom who was under such a curse. A girl with flame-red hair who was imprisoned in a tower. Wild Rose took in the mother's tearful fern-green eyes, the father's sunset hair, the little girl's determined quest for freedom. And she knew without a doubt that the bear family's stolen daughter was Aurelia.

PART THREE

SILVERTHORNE RISING

And the day came when the risk to remain tight in a bud was more painful than the risk it took to blossom.

Anonymous

THE THIRD TALE

The Stolen Daughter

At the edge of a fathomless forest, in a castle the colour of bone, a baby was born at the stroke of midnight. But, alas, all was not well.

'She's dead,' the young mother gasped, her tumbling hair plastered to her brow, her voice as bitter as winter frost. She staggered from her chamber. Wrapped in a cloak of deepest red, she ran across the snowy courtyard to where the huntsman stood and pushed her bundle into his arms.

'The child is dead,' she whispered. 'Please take her away. Hide our shame.'

The young mother returned to her castle and implored her husband to help her. For the kingdom must have a princess . . . They had all been waiting for many years, and the queen was yet to bear an heir. The worried king sent the Royal Guard into every village, searching for a newborn baby girl.

And so it happened that in the village of Silverdel, in a modest home, a baby had been born at the last minute of midnight.

'She's perfect!' cried her mother, her dark, tumbling hair pushed back from her brow. Her green eyes as bright as the ferns by the river.

The proud new father lit lanterns and hung a banner of joy in the window, woven from hemp and nettle, announcing their daughter's name: *Briar*.

Somewhere a window was open, letting in a snow-laced wind. It skittered through the cottage, full of mischief, carrying away the scent of happy tears, and the sound of the tiniest, tenderest whimper, soft as a nightingale's wing.

The local wise woman, who lived with her husband in the Ebony House on the brink of the forest and who had helped bring the child into the world, bid the young family farewell as they settled down for their first night together.

But no sooner had the babe begun to cry than a swift, echoing knock sounded at the door.

'Who could it be at this late hour?' asked the father.

'Well-wishers,' said the mother, beaming, and she rose on trembling legs, laid the baby carefully in her crib and opened the door, her face radiant with joy.

Three of the Royal Guard stood upon the doorstep, their expressions grave, their swords drawn.

'Can we help you?' asked the young mother, suddenly afraid.

The guards bowed once, low and sorrowfully. 'My lady, we have come for the child.'

The mother was still, not understanding. 'What do you mean?' she asked, confused.

But the guards pushed her aside and strode into the cottage. The father leaped up, shielding his child with all his strength. But the Royal Guard were ruthless, and it seemed the young father would soon die at their hands.

The mother, consumed with rage, seized her diamond-hilt sword – a family heirloom – and fought the guards off. But the sword was far deadlier than she knew and soon two of the Royal Guard lay slain on the cottage floor.

She screamed and dropped the sword. Her poor husband ran to her. Together they turned to their daughter's crib, but found it was empty.

The third guard had stolen their beloved child.

The heartbroken husband jumped upon his horse and rode through the wild, snowy night, all the way to the castle. But he was stopped at the drawbridge and though he fought hard, and even tried to swim across the moat, his life was threatened and he was forced to turn back.

The desperate young mother, numb with shock and grief, stumbled from her cottage and hurried to the Ebony House on the edge of the woods, the thickly falling flakes of snow covering her tracks.

'Help me,' she begged, and the wise woman let her in.

Many things unfolded that dark winter's night in the Ebony House.

The blood was scrubbed from the mother's hands and her nerves were soothed with lemon balm. Her husband arrived, empty-handed and hollow-faced.

The huntsman returned home to his wife, having left a baby crowned in lavender in the care of the wolves. Finally, then, they sat down and formed a plan.

It was only the lone pearl moon and a watchful owl that saw the huntsman ride solemnly away. Deep into Silverthorne Forest he fled on a mare the colour of mist. Through tangled briars, over shifting rocks and rushing brooks, never pausing.

For a forest can hold many secrets. Promises murmured beneath a new moon. Pathways so twisted they defy any map. Dark truths hidden in the heart of a wolf. There are many strange tales that weave through a wood, and Silverthorne Forest was no exception.

For the second time that midwinter's night, the huntsman reached a glade of trembling aspen and alder buckthorn, still rich with dark berries. He tethered his horse to a slanting silver birch and knocked boldly upon a hidden door. And there he stood among glittering shadows, until a man with a blue-black beard gruffly came to the door.

For the second time, the huntsman stood solid and still as he told the Folk of the Forest his story, hoping with all his heart that they'd help.

And being honourable people who hated the queen, the same cruel queen who let them stay in the forest for the heavy price of working in the mines, the men and women agreed again to help. So, by moonlight and mist, another pact was made. A pact to save the stolen baby and help the family escape the queen's wrath.

The plan was called *the Rising*.

When the day of the princess's christening came, the Rising was ready.

But before the huntsman could give the signal, before the Forest Folk could attack from the trees, before the guardswomen could steal back the baby, everyone at the palace sank to the floor in slumber.

When they all awoke, they learned of Dormevega, the wicked fairy, and the terrible curse.

So baby Briar was not taken back. She was instead christened Aurelia, cursed and imprisoned in an unreachable tower.

In the heart of the forest, her parents wept bitterly.

They could not return to Silverdel because of the guards who had died by the diamond-hilt sword. So the Forest Folk, the wise woman and the apothecary helped them find a new home in the Wild Wood. A home scorched with fire so it looked uninhabitable.

Here they would wait until the curse had been broken, then they would finally rescue their daughter.

The Rising remained in waiting.

As the years spun by and the seasons changed, the couple never forgot their stolen child. But they did grow to know happiness and peace once more and, with time, they had another daughter.

A little girl who was drawn to the forest like a bird to the sky. Its wild boughs and dancing leaves whispering their way through her childhood, haunting her every dream.

And on nights when the moon is high in the vast wintry skies, among the howl of wolves, she hears singing.

A voice bright as bone, wild as a wolf. Singing a melody of moonlight and freedom.

CHAPTER TWENTY-ONE

Midwinter Dreams

ild Rose rode away from the three bears' cottage in a state of wonder and fury.

Aurelia is their daughter. Her real name is Briar.

The shock of it stunned her like a bolt of lightning. It seemed impossible. And yet.

Wild Rose had grown up in a forest of impossible reality. She knew the very rhythm of life was full of surprises so sharp they could kill you. And though her heart beat with hope to have found Aurelia's true family, and outrage that the king and queen had taken her, a question hummed at the back of her mind.

Why would the king and queen steal a baby?

In all her years of study with the Lady Mal, Wild Rose had witnessed the occasional distraught young woman who had come to the apothecary to beg for a tonic to help a baby bloom. Surely the queen could have done the same?

Perhaps the queen's baby died . . .

Something made her stop and sit bolt upright on the little grey horse, who obeyed perfectly and halted mid-step. A coldness pressed against Wild Rose's heart, the woods suddenly looked jagged, and a sense of foreboding clung to the air. She shook herself free of the feeling and willed it to float away on the breeze.

The woods were once again illuminated by the golden glow of winter sunshine and the air was crisp and bright, but her heart still beat out of rhythm. The day was almost over. She had four days left to help Aurelia escape.

She did not go home but galloped swiftly to the Lady Mal's house. If anyone knew about the secrets of the castle and the forest, it was the apothecary. But Wild Rose arrived at an empty garden: the Lady Mal wasn't at home. This was not unusual. The hour was late and the Lady Mal was often called away on errands at the castle or beyond.

Wild Rose slipped lightly from the horse's back and set her loose to wander in the secluded walled garden.

Witch light bathed the garden in a hue of silver-gold, and Wild Rose drew her scarlet cloak about her and curled up in a dry, snowless spot beneath the boughs of the largest pine tree to wait for the Lady Mal's return.

Sleep found Wild Rose, but her dreams were strange and ominous. She awoke, breathless and shivering, wishing for her wolves.

She had dreamed of lost children. Like the little frozen boy who couldn't hear. There had been others throughout the years, each with something that set them apart in the eyes of the village.

Don't think of them now.

She pushed the dream away and emerged into the evening starlight to find the apothecary's black stallion and her misty mare side by side, contentedly munching thistles.

Wild Rose turned towards the welcome light of the Lady Mal's home, darted down the path and knocked three times on the secret side door. There came a light stirring of silk slippers over stone, then a welcoming squeak as the door creaked open. Before Wild Rose, in the flickering of candlelight, stood Lady Mal.

'I thought that petulant little horse might belong to you,' came her voice, soft as summer rain.

Wild Rose grinned. 'Of course.'

'And were you going to ask permission to keep her in my garden?' chimed the apothecary playfully.

'I'm here now, aren't I?' Wild Rose beamed at her.

The Lady Mal tutted lightly. 'Come inside and have some soup. You'll have missed supper with your family.'

Wild Rose nodded gratefully and followed her into the room with the high ceiling. A fire burned fiercely, and several cauldrons bubbled and steamed. She was determined to ask about the family of bears, find out exactly what had happened to Aurelia . . . and yet something made her pause. Maybe she just wanted to enjoy the welcome comfort of the Lady Mal's home after the strangeness of her dream.

'Pour two bowls from the smallest pot.'

Wild Rose dutifully took a couple of bowls and filled each one with a heartening broth of courgette, mint and potato. It smelled of her childhood and the cosiness of long winter nights filled with warmth.

As she ladled out the soup, Wild Rose glanced at the other bubbling pots.

'Which spells are you concocting now?' she asked.

'The usual ones I brew at night,' replied the Lady Mal, seating herself in a high-backed chair by the long window.

The apothecary was interrupted by a terrible pounding that rattled the walls. She went rigid.

'The Royal Guard. Or worse,' she hissed, seizing Wild Rose by the hood of her cloak and hurrying her into a large pantry. 'Stay hidden and don't make a sound.' Then the cupboard doors closed, extinguishing the light, and Wild Rose was alone in the airless pitch-black.

A crack of light shone through the join of the doors, and Wild Rose pressed her eye to it, holding her breath and watching with heightened alertness as the Lady Mal swirled the soup bowls into the sink, smoothed down her skirts, raised her head and went to open the door.

As the visitor swept into the room, Wild Rose spied that it was not the Royal Guard who had come to call but Queen Evaline herself.

Wild Rose had only seen the queen and her royal escorts ride through the forest once. They had escorted the queen to the Lady Mal's home, loitering on nervous horses near the entrance, waiting uneasily for the queen. Wild Rose had watched unseen and intrigued from the high branches.

Her family had been frantic with worry. Worry for her and the wolves. Wild Rose shared their fear but didn't understand it.

'Forgive the intrusion, Witch of the Woods,' came a sharp voice.

'I'm an apothecary, not a witch – as you well know, Your Majesty – and you are quite forgiven,' answered the Lady Mal a little tersely.

Wild Rose smiled in the gloomy darkness. The Lady Mal always maintained such arresting authority; it really was like magic.

'I cannot sleep,' said the queen, sounding ragged. 'Nothing works: not wine, nor whisky and, even if sleep comes, my dreams are so strange. You must do something. Anything.'

She was advancing towards the Lady Mal, her eyes manic, darting. Wild Rose had never seen hair so silver, nor lips so red, nor eyes so wild . . .

'The Dreamer's Draught is almost ready.'

'How did you know I would come?' murmured the queen in a low, dangerous tone.

'I did not know for certain,' said the Lady Mal, shrugging. 'You never sleep well near midwinter. One dose and you will find peace again.'

'That is what you say every time,' replied the queen thinly, and Wild Rose felt a beat of dread pulse through the air.

Was the queen threatening the Lady Mal?

In all her years, Wild Rose had never heard anything kind about the queen. Her uncles and aunts spoke of her in hushed, troubled voices. The queen's stolen daughter, Aurelia, didn't trust her. And the bear family seemed to live in total fear of her. Up close, the queen looked like a maiden cut from ice, all sharp edges and angles, hair so bright it could have been spun from a star.

She sank wretchedly into a chair. 'Why is it I am cursed with this nightmare? I have protected my thankless daughter. I have given her everything. Why do I dream it is not so?'

'We cannot know the workings of the mind,' the Lady Mal said smoothly. 'I suspect it is what comes with great responsibility. You are a queen and a mother; both roles require sacrifice. You must be kind to yourself.'

The queen murmured something inaudible and Wild Rose realized she was weeping. Not sobbing with sorrow, but trembling with tears of rage.

'I will not be plagued by this spiteful dream any longer. Give me the potion at once,' hissed the queen, rising quick as a snake and glowering at the Lady Mal.

Wild Rose swallowed down her fears, wondering what would happen if the apothecary couldn't meet the queen's wishes. The Lady Mal was an astonishing woman, living alone in the woods, but it would be so easy for the queen to claim she really was a witch . . . and then the villagers' tolerance of her would end.

'It is just brewed,' answered the Lady Mal as there came a sound of thick liquid bubbling and pouring, then the smoky smell of the fire going out. Then a clinking of silver.

'You will ride with me to the fallen sycamore where my guard awaits, and you will speak of this to no one.'

'As you wish,' said the Lady Mal.

Wild Rose listened to the swirling swish of light feet over the stone floor, then the click of the door closing and the thick, breathing silence that followed.

Pressing her ear to the cupboard doors, she waited for other sounds, but there was only the thrum of her own racing heart. A slow sigh escaped her lips. She stumbled backwards, trying to push the doors fully open, and almost collided with a deadly spike. Catching herself not a moment too soon, Wild Rose spun away from the odd contraption and flung the doors wide.

She gave a gasp of alarm to see that, whatever the strange thing was, it had left a tiny rip in her scarlet cloak. She glared at the cupboard crossly as a stream of moonlight flooded in and Wild Rose saw what had almost harmed her.

It was circular and seemed to be part wheel, part pedal, with a point as sharp as a diamond. Wild Rose had never seen anything like it. But she sensed the wrongness of it all the same.

A wheel . . . a spinning wheel. A spinning wheel with a spindle!

The Lady Mal must have kept one in secret after King Aspen abolished them to protect Aurelia. Wild Rose touched the river pearl at her throat, thinking of her beloved friend.

Why was a spinning wheel here? Did the Lady Mal know Dormevega, the wicked fairy?

A thousand uncertain thoughts swished and swirled through Wild Rose's mind. But one thing was certain – here was an object that had the power to destroy Aurelia's hopes of escaping her curse and changing her future. Rose knew she couldn't just leave the spindle now she had discovered it.

She ought to burn it . . .

But what if it's connected to the curse?

Perhaps she could keep it in the forest, hidden underground?

But what if someone finds it?

Maybe she could ask the Forest Folk to hide it.

But what if it brings them harm?

What if it were thrown into the River Spell?

But anyone could find it and use it to hurt Aurelia . . .

Wild Rose gave a small gasp as she realized the only safe place for the spindle was with Aurelia herself. Where no one would ever think to look.

And then a new thought drifted slyly through her mind.

Maybe it could help Aurelia to understand the curse . . .

Without giving herself a chance to lose her nerve, Wild Rose seized a little lantern and struck a flame from a block of flint.

By the light of the lantern, she very delicately placed her fingers round the narrowest part of the spindle, avoiding the spike, and twisted and wiggled it until at last, with a final tug, it came loose. Ever so carefully, she placed it deep in the folds of her pocket.

Then she was flying out of the Lady Mal's house, the lantern held before her like a talisman to ward off evil. Within heartbeats, she was upon the little grey horse and through the garden, up the stairs and riding into the night. The scarlet cloak billowed out behind her like a cape of blood.

As they galloped through the moonstruck dark, wolves fell into step with them, then peeled off towards their own bright-eyed adventures. Night birds called hauntingly through the air. A dark-winged moth danced helplessly towards the lantern's flame. A red fox darted clear of their path, its eyes huge and searching.

Reaching the fire tree, Wild Rose tethered her precious horse – whom she was becoming increasingly fond of – to it. She whistled then as she waited, leaning into the little animal, breathing her scent of mist and apples, until a wolf with dappled fur came prowling from the trees.

Wild Rose knelt down carefully, aware of the spindle in her pocket. She looked deep into her wolf's eyes. Lullaby gazed back with a loyalty brighter than starlight, and Wild Rose found herself beaming with fierce, feral love.

'You must guard my horse. Let nothing harm her.' The wolf gave a low growl, a begrudging agreement. 'I won't be long, I promise.'

She rubbed her brow against Lullaby's and the wolf licked Wild Rose's face, then tilted her snout to the sky and howled. The scarlet-clad girl joined in, their voices rising in perfect harmony.

Beyond the Spindle Wood and across the deep moat, a girl in a tower awoke and flew wide-eyed to her window.

CHAPTER TWENTY-TWO

The Spindle, the Wings and the Spell

Dark clouds skittered past the moon, a voice rang out bright as bone and a princess leaned from her tower and let down a rope made of her own red hair. Aurelia's face was lit with the radiance of hope. Wild Rose didn't even need the owl call.

Wild Rose took off her scarlet cloak, quickly drawing something sharp and glittery from its pocket and clasped it in her teeth. Then she hid her cloak and boots in the dry tree hollow and dived into the moat like a mermaid returning to the sea.

Aurelia held her breath while Wild Rose was underwater, only daring to gasp when the pale-faced girl bobbed to the surface, her hair slick to her skin. And, in those moments, Aurelia had never felt so grateful to be alive, so full of wonder at this wild girl with star-bright hair who was scaling her walls with the promise of friendship.

Wild Rose ascended the tower so quickly Aurelia was astounded. There seemed to be no method to it, just agility and determination. Though she scrambled and slipped, Wild Rose never gave up her grasp on the rope, winding it round her elbow and knees, clasping it with her fist.

'Come in!' cried Aurelia, opening her arms in welcome as Wild Rose triumphantly reached the windowsill. But the wild girl held up her hand in warning, pausing on the sill in a catlike crouch, her shadow blocking out the moon, the silver point gleaming wickedly between her teeth.

Carefully she took the sharpened hook from her mouth and pointed its blade-like edge towards the floor.

'Don't come any closer,' said Wild Rose, panting.

'Why?' asked the princess, regarding her strangely.

'I've got so much to tell you,' Wild Rose explained. 'About a family who live in the forest, about your mother, I mean the queen, and about something wicked I found by mistake in the apothecary's cupboard. A spindle.'

Aurelia shot backwards into the curve of the wall, touching its cool, solid circumference for protection.

'Why did you bring it here?' she asked, looking aghast.

'Don't be afraid. I can throw it in the moat right now if it frightens you. But if you do wish to break the curse, maybe this will help us?'

Aurelia stared at her, half terrified, half transfixed.

'I don't understand why the Lady Mal has it.'

Wild Rose sighed. 'She must have kept it secretly after the king banished them, but I couldn't just leave it there. And I couldn't risk hiding it in the forest . . . It's safest here with you. We'll put it in a box and conceal it somewhere unreachable.'

'Swear you won't let it touch me?' Aurelia continued.

'I swear by the light of the moon and my beating heart.'

Aurelia smiled and stepped away from the wall.

'Now where can I put it that's safe?' asked Wild Rose.

'In the birdcage!' Aurelia cried, gesturing at once to the empty gilt cage.

'Where's the blue bird?'

'I set him free. He really wasn't happy. And I'll be leaving the tower soon.'

'Aurelia, there's so much to say,' Wild Rose said breathlessly, hopping down and crossing the large room, leaving a trail of moat water. She placed the lethal-looking spindle inside the golden bars, shut the cage door and closed its ruby clasp. 'I hardly know where to start.'

'Well, I've got nowhere to go,' said Aurelia, in the playful tone her guardswomen used. 'I'll light every candle and the fire. And I'll heat some fresh tea and then you can tell me everything.'

Wild Rose nodded, and helped to light the room.

'Here,' said Aurelia, noticing that Wild Rose was starting to shiver. 'Put this on and I'll dry your clothes by the fire.' And she held out an old dress that was the pale blue of summer skies.

Wild Rose smiled and slipped the dress on gratefully. She had never known anything as lovely – it felt like wearing blossom.

'Thank you, Your Majesty,' she said in jest, sinking into a curtsy.

Aurelia glanced at her and caught her breath. The dress made the wild girl look most bewitching. Her face was snow-white, her lips blood-red and her eyes were the blue of mountain rivers in winter.

'*You* look like the princess now,' Aurelia giggled, returning the curtsy. But there was such a sharpness to Wild Rose's features that Aurelia corrected herself. 'No, you look like a queen. The Queen of Ice and Winter.'

Wild Rose swept towards her and clasped Aurelia's hands and they settled down beside the fire. Wild Rose thought, *How to begin?* How could she possibly weave everything together in a way that made sense? She thought of the stories Jeremiah, Tobias and Oak used to tell her, and how they made her feel safe as well as full of courage. The forest folklore was in her blood – she just needed to trust in herself. She took a breath and, a little nervously, began the story . . .

'Once, long ago, on a cold winter's night, a lovely couple had a baby girl. But no sooner had they named her than the Royal Guard banged on their door and stole the child away, taking her to Silverthorne Castle.'

Aurelia's breath stilled and she leaned forward. 'Why?'

'On that very same night, the young and beautiful queen had also given birth to a child – who died.'

Aurelia drew back in alarm. 'Died?'

Wild Rose shrugged and let go of Aurelia's hands. 'I think.'

There was a moment's silence. Then Wild Rose continued.

'The stolen baby was given to Queen Evaline and King Aspen. And the lovely couple, heartbroken by grief, ran away to the forest to live in disguise, waiting for the day they could steal their daughter back.'

Aurelia shook her head in confusion. 'But where's the baby now? Is she in the castle?'

Wild Rose bit her lip. 'The king and queen changed her name. They told the world she was their daughter.'

Time seemed to cease and sounds seemed to stop. It was as if Aurelia were in a dream, crossing the threshold of an alternate reality.

'They pretended she was their princess.'

And, with that, Aurelia tipped into that new reality: a different understanding of the world. All at once, her thoughts rushed together, then drew apart in a different order, until she finally understood.

Her mother's disapproval. Her father's mistrust. Her much younger brother's disinterest. Her sunset hair.

'I'm the stolen baby.' And suddenly she knew it was true, the same way she knew that birdsong signals dawn.

Wild Rose solemnly nodded, letting the story settle. 'Your true family lives in the forest disguised as bears,' she said at last. 'They long to free you and take you to safety.'

Aurelia's hands flew to her mouth. A deep frown etched upon her brow. 'Why haven't they rescued me? Why haven't they tried?' she asked.

'The curse,' said Wild Rose as gently as she could. 'They are just as afraid of it as the king and queen.'

Aurelia shot to her feet, quite furious. 'Damn this wretched curse!' she seethed. She began stamping round the room and kicking the doors of her cupboard.

Wild Rose ran to her side, putting her hand to Aurelia's cheek. 'We will break it. We'll find a way.'

'But how?' Aurelia whispered, shimmering with rage.

'I don't know yet. But look at everything that's already happened. I dreamed of leaving the forest; you longed for freedom. I crossed under impassable thorn bushes, and swam through the moat. You made a rope from spun hair. You crafted wings from hope and feathers, and somehow, in spite of everything, we met. We have to believe we can change your fate. Because, Aurelia, you've already changed mine.'

Aurelia threw her arms round Wild Rose and hugged her as if she might never let go. Then she pushed her sunset locks out of her face and dried her eyes, focusing her gaze on the spindle in the gilded cage.

'You were right to bring it here,' she said softly. 'We have to understand the curse so we can find a way to break it.'

'Should we try to test it?' asked Wild Rose.

Aurelia nodded carefully, unfastening the ruby catch, but before she had time to think, Wild Rose was reaching into the gilt cage and touching the spike of the spindle.

A drop of scarlet blood hit the floor. A candle flickered to smoke. The wind sang its sad winter lullaby.

But otherwise nothing happened and the two girls gazed at each other.

'So we know I'm immune to its curse.' Wild Rose chuckled.

'But what if you hadn't been!' Aurelia cried, looking cross, but Wild Rose only laughed.

'Let's both cut a lock of hair and see if anything happens,' she suggested instead.

Neither lock, when held to the spindle, reacted in any way.

Next they tried a shred of nail from each of their littlest fingers, then an eyelash, and even a drop of Aurelia's blood dripped on to the spindle, after one of her pink-winged doves obediently pecked her.

They tried scorching the spindle with fire and repeated every experiment again, then they dipped it in rainwater, held it up to the moon, sprinkled it with cinnamon and arrowroot and used it to crush a garlic clove. Still nothing happened.

'The thing I don't understand about the curse,' Wild Rose said as they stood by the window, sipping ginger and cardamom tea, 'is if you need true love's kiss to break it then you'd have to love the person who kisses you – as well as them loving you.'

'Yes.' Aurelia nodded.

'So couldn't the king or queen awaken you with a kiss?' But, even as she spoke the words, Wild Rose knew the answer.

They don't love her and she doesn't love them.

'Well, *I* love you,' Wild Rose said loyally.

Aurelia stared at her silently for a long while. 'Then that's it . . .' she said at last.

Wild Rose looked at her intently and Aurelia began backing away from her towards the birdcage, tears hovering on the curve of her cheek.

'If it works . . . you must wake me. You can break the curse. Promise me.'

Wild Rose frowned, but before she could even blink Aurelia was reaching into the gilt bars, her finger touching the sharp spike of the spindle.

A drop of scarlet blood hit the floor. A candle flickered to smoke. The wind sang its sad winter lullaby.

Aurelia swayed for a moment, her eyes fluttering wildly. Wild Rose was beside her in moments, holding out her arms to catch her if she fell. But she didn't.

The two girls stared at each other, their mouths falling open at the miracle of it.

'The curse . . . it must be broken!' Aurelia gasped. Then they were screaming, whooping, stampeding round the circular room like untamed horses.

Wild Rose suddenly stood still.

'What is it?' asked Aurelia.

Wild Rose turned to face the princess, her blue eyes glinting. 'That seemed so easy, don't you think?'

Aurelia froze. 'What do you mean?'

'If you'd been cursed by a powerful fairy, wouldn't it take more than me just telling you I loved you to break it? Maybe . . . maybe you never were cursed?'

Aurelia looked ashen. 'You mean because I'm not really the princess?'

Wild Rose considered this a moment, then shook her head. 'What if the entire thing is made up?'

'But the queen saw the wicked fairy lay the curse on me herself.'

'Maybe so,' Wild Rose said darkly. She was still thinking. 'I was at the Lady Mal's this evening, and the queen came by.'

Aurelia frowned in confusion. 'My mother went to the apothecary's home? In the forest? At night? Why?'

'Nightmares, she said. Something she half remembers. Probably the sadness of her own child dying and the guilt of stealing you. And maybe the guilt of fooling the whole kingdom into thinking you were cursed by sending them to sleep and keeping you locked in a tower . . .'

'So the queen knew of a sleeping spell?'

'Yes. It's called the Dreamer's Draught. It's very powerful. And the queen is the only one who says she remembers the curse being cast,' Wild Rose whispered. 'Do you think she enchanted the whole kingdom?'

Aurelia shook her head. 'Why would she do such an evil thing?'

'To keep you in her power . . . so your true family couldn't steal you back,' Wild Rose added very gently.

'But why couldn't they just have had another child instead? Why did they need to steal me? Nothing makes sense.'

Wild Rose did know the answer to this, for even rumours can spread to a forest.

'The queen's child *was* long awaited. Perhaps she couldn't face the shame of Silverthorne never having an heir?'

Aurelia gave a long, fretful sigh, balled her fists and wept.

Wild Rose threw her arms round the princess, drawing her into a close hug as Aurelia trembled and sobbed.

'I must fetch my wings. I want to leave right now. Tonight!'

Wild Rose held Aurelia's hands between her own and her little arm. 'But if this is true – that the curse is a lie – it still doesn't mean you're free. The queen will come after you and your family. She will hunt the whole forest to protect herself. We have to be clever.'

Aurelia bared her teeth against the bitter taste of resentment, but knew that Wild Rose was right. 'Fine. What do I need to do?'

'I think I have an idea. But we would have to wait until the night of the Midwinter Ball – can you do that?'

'Three whole days stuck in this wretched place?'

'*Only* three days,' said Wild Rose.

'And then?' asked Aurelia, the thrill of excitement taking hold.

'We will still need your beautiful wings and the spindle, and the Dreamer's Draught.'

'Tell me everything,' Aurelia murmured.

Together they blew out every candle and dulled the fire to a low flame. For a scheme of such secrecy and importance needed to be cloaked in darkness. They talked and talked, until they were certain that they had thought of everything they possibly could. A nightingale trilled through the sky and they smiled, their hearts set.

'Will you be able to cross the moat?' Aurelia asked, slipping the wings carefully on to Wild Rose's back.

The effect was instant. With her bedraggled hair and icy eyes, she looked like a girl born of black swans.

'Of course,' said Wild Rose as Aurelia fastened the spindle to the sash of Wild Rose's dress.

The two girls embraced as hard as they could, the wings brushing against them.

As Aurelia let down her bright auburn rope of hair, she refused to cry. She watched with bated breath as

Wild Rose angled the wings carefully out of the window, slid down the long rope, then reached the moat and began to swim powerfully across it.

At first, all was well. But soon the weight of the wings caused them to dip beneath the surface. And, once wet and waterlogged, they began dragging Wild Rose down. Aurelia's heart stopped. But, despite being repeatedly pulled under, Wild Rose's determination kept her resurfacing, and pushing on, until finally she reached the far side.

As Wild Rose heaved herself up the bank, the white wolf appeared, seizing one of the wings in her teeth and half yanking the girl out of the moat. She clambered to her feet, water running off her, and pressed her forehead to the wolf's.

Aurelia did not take her eyes from Wild Rose, watching as she swapped the wings for the cloak, clutching the wet feathers in her arms. Then she turned and gave a single hopeful wave before vanishing with her wolf into the dark.

But neither of them saw the sleepless boy by the moat's edge watching the girl with the wings and the wolf. He smiled wickedly. His lips savage red, his skin pale as snow, his hair the silver-bright of a star.

CHAPTER TWENTY-THREE

Find Me at First Light

Deep in the heart of the night-dark forest a scarlet-clad girl rode upon a grey horse. Great wings were draped across the little filly's back so the night wind might dry them. Had you caught a glimpse of their shadow, you might have thought them the stuff of legends.

She had no light, for she knew the twisted paths of the forest as well as the lines that criss-crossed her palm. Great trees drew back their gnarled boughs for her, stars realigned to gleam for her, the moon beamed down in celestial warning, but the girl just tipped her face to the vast, endless sky and howled, feral and sweet.

She was wilder than the first snow on a winter's morn. Wilder than moonlight on a midsummer's eve.

Wilder than midnight in a fathomless forest.

This was a girl with the heart of a wolf. And a plan as cunning as a wicked fairy's.

If their scheme were truly going to work, they needed the help of someone who knew both the forest and the castle, someone who could slip between worlds as easily as the Lady Mal, but far less noticeable. Someone they could trust.

They needed Saffron of Silverdel.

The little grey horse sped through the Wild Wood, until finally they came to the edge of the forest. A place where the sky was endless and wide, and the world was empty of trees.

Wild Rose had never set foot near the village of Silverdel. Years of the Forest Folk's warnings rang in her ears, but she closed her mind to them, as she did to the cold wind, and rode on.

Reaching the oak tree swing, where she had waved farewell to Verity just hours earlier, Wild Rose paused on the threshold of her forest, her home, her safety. Drawing her scarlet cloak round her, she slipped soundlessly from the little filly's back, quietly tethering her to the oak tree, laid the wings across the bough of a large fir tree, then crept as lightly as thistledown out of the shadow of the woods.

The Ebony House was bathed in darkness but for a single luminous lantern hanging over its doorway, a welcome beam of light for lost travellers. But Wild Rose did not approach the door. She stole into the winter garden, breathing in the lingering scent of lilac and camomile as she scaled a snowy pear tree.

She had no idea how to signal to Saffy, but thinking of the first time she had ever seen her, wandering through the woods with a basket on her arm, Wild Rose remembered Saffy's affinity with birds – how she had called them down effortlessly from the sky. Wild Rose took a breath of crisp night air and called three times like an owl.

At first, nothing happened and Wild Rose silently cursed. She closed her eyes and listened hard, but the house gave away no secrets.

She called again, louder. And this time she was sure she sensed the stirring of blankets. A light flickered on and somewhere within a baby started crying.

Had she woken the entire family?

Quickly Wild Rose withdrew into the branches of the tree, hoping the dark would keep her hidden. Then, to her amazement, she saw Saffy's curious face appear in a little window at the very top of the house. Wild Rose dropped to the snowy ground and moved ever so lightly into the gleam of the lantern, her hood pushed back, her face raised to the moon.

Saffy's brown eyes opened wide with wonderment as Wild Rose beckoned to her before moving to the bottom of the garden.

After what seemed like an eternity, Saffy emerged, bright-cheeked and delighted, her deep blue snowflake cloak thrown hurriedly over her nightgown, a chubby, cross-faced baby wrapped in her arms. Wild Rose had never seen a baby up close before and she couldn't keep from smiling at the very joy of him.

'He's a terrible sleeper,' Saffy whispered. 'My parents think I'm taking him for a walk round the garden – I have to be quick.' Then she frowned. 'Your hair's wet – are you all right?'

'I'm fine. I've come from the castle. Walk with me to the swing. There's much to say.'

And, as they walked, they whispered, and the baby fretted and grumbled. By the time Wild Rose had finished telling her tale, Saffy felt as if she'd been struck by a bolt of lightning. The truth of so much twisted folklore unravelling at once stunned her into silence.

'We need your help, Saffy,' Wild Rose said urgently, leaning in close to the girl and the baby in order to share the secret plan.

Saffy blinked at the wild girl in admiration and shock, then slowly nodded. 'I'm sure I can get the ingredients for the Dreamer's Draught. It must be in one of my mother's spell books. There's nothing she doesn't know.' She paused, staring at Wild Rose with breathtaking hopefulness. 'Do you think it will work?'

Wild Rose gave a gleaming grin in answer. 'And you will help us on the night of the ball?'

Saffy sank into a low and graceful curtsy. 'But of course,' she said, smiling mischievously.

The baby moaned and wriggled. The two friends giggled with the quiet elation of adventures to come. Wild Rose kissed the baby on his cross little cheek and they parted ways – Saffy hurrying back inside the Ebony House, Wild Rose returning to her beloved forest home.

Reaching the tunnel of hawthorn, Wild Rose cantered straight down it, the spindle clipped at her waist glinting in the starlight. Near the half-burnt cottage, she brought the horse to a standstill and whistled shrilly.

At first, there was only the wind and the distant call of a gliding owl. Wild Rose closed her eyes, sensing the darkness beyond the cottage door, and there she felt a soft, wakeful stirring.

There was a scuffle and a gasp. A child's face appeared at the window, then vanished, snatched away by a worried parent.

'Do not be afraid!' she called, making her voice carry as the Lady Mal had taught her, imagining it echoing right up to the moon.

There came the whispered sound of swearing, then the door swung violently open and a man – the father – advanced, holding a dagger, the bear head set over his own, its black eyes like pearls in the dark.

He faltered slightly at the sight of the crimson-cloaked girl upon a young horse beneath the snow-kissed magnolia tree.

Wild Rose sat up straight. 'I have news of your stolen daughter. Come to the Forest Folk's glade at first light and I will tell you everything.'

The father staggered back slightly, the dagger falling from his hand, and his wife pushed past him, her bear head raised, her green eyes bright as the ferns that grow by the river.

'Who are you?' she gasped as Wild Rose turned the little grey horse round and crossed the garden. She paused at the tunnel and lowered her scarlet hood. Moonlight illuminated her fair hair, giving it the pale iridescence of a dragonfly's wing.

'It's Wild Rose!' cried a gleeful voice. And there, dancing in the garden, her bear-like shadow silhouetted by the moon, was Aurelia's little sister, Hester.

Wild Rose beamed at the girl, then geed her horse into a gallop and vanished through the tunnel of hawthorn.

She did not hear the mother call out in dismay, nor see the father drop to his knees in despair. She only saw the littlest bear spinning through the dark in heart-struck awe.

So she galloped on through the tangled forest towards the Lady Mal's home. Her velvet cloak pushed back over her shoulders, the night wind drying the dress Aurelia had gifted her. It was so much lighter than her usual clothes, fluttering against her skin.

Like a princess, Wild Rose thought.

She did not enter the Lady Mal's walled garden, but rapped boldly with the devil-horned knocker. When the apothecary emerged, Wild Rose spoke again with the assured tone the Lady Mal herself had taught her: 'Come to the Forest Folk's glade by first light. I have news of the princess.'

Then she cantered away, not looking back. Wolves melted out of the wilderness, brutally graceful as they matched pace with the little grey horse and filled the forest with their howls.

Soon they came to a place so dark the air itself was ebony: a glade of trembling aspen and alder buckthorn, still rich with dark berries, where a tumbledown home lay in darkness.

The wolves slunk into the undergrowth, camouflaging all but their golden eyes. It seemed like the forest was full of fallen stars.

Wild Rose straightened, pausing to breathe in the cool wind. It carried the scent of her home. An aroma like honey and thistles and wolf fur, mixed with a hint of adventure. And suddenly she felt the rising sensation that everything was about to change. She reached up into the branches of an alder tree and tugged at a hanging conker.

A tiny bell rang out through the Deep Wood, its chime tuneful and sweet. It was impossible to tell where the chime came from because, in fact, there were many little silver bells hidden in hollows or woven through hedges, all linked by thin interconnecting twine. A melody of Fae magic spilling through the mist. Summoning Wild Rose's family.

She watched in restless silence as a light flickered on in her family's home and the wolf pack rose to their feet. They moved in formation, like part of a dance, forming a horseshoe round the edge of the glade with Wild Rose in the space at the top.

As the Forest Folk came stumbling into the dark, carrying lanterns of pumpkins and squash carved with the pattern of stars, they made their way towards each of their wolves. Or perhaps each beast made its way towards a specific person. It was hard to tell, but soon enough they were all gathered beneath the silver birch. Each one protected, and each wolf with its guardian.

Oak, with her fine knowledge of the forest and her wolf named for her rare maple-leaf fur: Red.

Jeremiah, the beloved storyteller, a fabulous poet and actor, wise in the subtlest of ways. Wisdom stood beside him, her sharp intelligence ever-glimmering like an aura.

Akina, speaker of many languages and writer of the most beautiful calligraphy. Heartless stood proudly at her side, large and black and silver.

Rivern, king of waterways, and his wolf, Evening Star, who was the silver-grey of starlight.

Etienne, with his flair for fabric and food. Petite Love, his multicoloured wolf of black, white and grey, moved tenderly round him.

Sailor, the most amazing singer, seemed to know every shanty in the land. Tempest, his mist-coloured wolf, stood before him, as wild as her name.

And Tobias – or Blackbeard – the protector of the group. With his rugged charm and worried eyes. Rogue, his one-eyed pup, the same dark shade as his beard.

As their gaze adjusted to the deepness of the night, the seven Folk of the Forest blinked in alarm to see a fair maiden upon a pale horse. Her crimson cloak was the colour of spilled wine and her gown was surely sewn from the soul of the river. A dark pearl glittered at her throat and her hair was strewn with icicles that glimmered like a crown. She was regal and terrifying and impossibly graceful.

'Wild Rose?' Jeremiah gasped, laying a hand upon Wisdom's back to steady himself. The wolf leaned into him and gave a low whine.

'Yes,' she answered calmly, her fingers twirling through the horse's grey mane, keeping the little filly peaceful inside the circle of wolves. Lullaby and Snow flanked them, their wild eyes burning, their hackles raised.

Hoofbeats filled the air as a new horse rode into the clearing, halting at the sight of the men and women and their wolves, and the girl with her crown of winter. The Lady Mal.

All eyes fell upon Wild Rose and a whispering hush descended.

'What is it, child?' asked Oak, feeling Red's fur bristle against her. Even as she said the last word, it felt wrong to her, seeming to snag in her throat.

'Where did you get such a gown?' asked Etienne, sounding impressed, Love giving a little yip of appreciation at his side.

'From a friend.'

'What friend?' growled Tobias, his expression murderous. 'Have you been talking to villagers again?'

'Not a villager,' said Wild Rose, her eyes serious and certain. 'A princess.'

An uproar broke out, a cacophony of shouts and howls, so no one could tell who was speaking and what was said.

Then a family of three bears stepped into this confusion, their bear heads pushed back, revealing two weary adults and the littlest girl whose face was wild with the prospect of adventure.

'What is going on?' whispered the mother.

The Forest Folk looked just as stunned to see the bear family.

Wild Rose reached for the spindle clipped at her waist, its point still stained with Aurelia's blood, and held it up for all to see.

'I know the truth,' she said simply. 'I know Aurelia isn't the real princess and she was stolen from you.' A deep silence ran round the glade as all regarded her with worried frowns. 'And I know the curse isn't real. The queen lied.'

'How can you know this?' asked the bear father, frowning at Wild Rose in sheer disbelief.

'Tonight I went to the castle, crossed the moat and climbed the tower.'

There were stifled gasps of horror, but the Lady Mal held up a hand to signal peace.

'The princess invited me – she let down a rope of her hair. She wanted me to help her escape so she could change her fate. I found a spindle . . .'

And here she glanced at the Lady Mal, who answered a little tersely. 'It was well hidden. I kept it for making twine only; no one has ever found it before.'

Everyone stared at her, quite taken aback. Apart from Tobias who looked at her with unflinching loyalty.

'And I too have to protect myself from the queen,' she said darkly. 'If she ever tried to harm me, the threat of a spindle would be my protection.' And this everyone understood.

Wild Rose turned to face the bear family now, her eyes so full of the story that she didn't notice the fear clouding their faces.

'When Aurelia learned that the queen had stolen her and she wasn't the true princess, she decided to test the curse. We agreed that if she did fall into a death-sleep I would waken her with true love's kiss.'

The mother bear swayed unsteadily, but nodded for Rose to continue.

'But I didn't need to because the curse was never real. The spindle wasn't enchanted. The queen created the fairy tale and made up the curse.'

Tobias dropped his axe with a heavy thud and put his hands over his eyes, tears streaming through them.

Akina and Rivern reached for each other's hands over their wolves.

Jeremiah laid a heavy hand upon his true love Etienne's shoulder.

They all looked bleak with worry.

Wild Rose gripped the little grey horse, and Lullaby and Snow both moved closer to her. Everyone's gaze seemed to burn her. She had expected them all to be relieved, even joyful at this news. The fearful curse was a lie. So why were they all so afraid?

She was getting the distinct sense that something was very, very wrong.

The bear mother stepped into the centre of the glade and addressed Wild Rose. 'Thank you for helping our girl. We are so grateful to you. But you must not return to the castle.'

Wild Rose felt her heart tighten.

'Do you know why the queen stole our daughter?' The mother's voice was whisper-thin.

Wild Rose couldn't find her words. When at last they came to her, her voice was hollow. 'The queen's baby died.'

The Folk of the Forest put their hands to their hearts, as if to keep them from breaking. The Lady Mal closed her eyes and took a sharp breath.

'No, my beloved girl,' said Tobias as softly as smoke. He strode forward, his eyes still wet, looking at her with all the love of a father. 'The queen's baby didn't die.'

The forest held its breath. Not even a snowflake stirred.

'You are the queen's real daughter.'

CHAPTER TWENTY-FOUR

Daughter of Wolves

A coldness pressed against Wild Rose's heart, as if she had swallowed ice. The woods suddenly felt jagged and sharp; the night air made her breathless.

For here was the truth she had somehow known. A truth she had turned away from. A truth that lived in the depths of her bones. In the place where echoes are made.

I would have been the princess. Aurelia would have had a family.

When her mother had been anonymous, she had seemed nothing more than a fairy tale. But now her mother had a name and a face, the same pale skin, star-spun hair and blood-red lips as Wild Rose herself. The truth was like a sword at her throat.

A single word chimed through her mind, demanding to be spoken.

Why?

But Wild Rose knew why the king and queen had given her up. For that answer too lived in the depths of her bones.

Because you were born with the Mark of the Witch.

Had she been alone, she might have screamed, or curled up in the warmth of Lullaby's fur, or stared at herself in the hanging mirror, trying to love herself through the pain. But she did none of these things.

There are no real witches. Only children born too different or folk who know too much.

Around her the larks called their dawn song, starlings dipped and swooped in flight and every golden eye of every wolf she'd ever loved gleamed at her fiercely.

Wild Rose blinked and came back to herself. The Forest Folk, the Lady Mal, her family of wolves and even the bears had their eyes fixed upon her, and it seemed that the moment might never end.

Then Hester spoke, her sweet little voice brimming with admiration. 'You're royalty!'

Wild Rose laughed, not bitterly but softly – with relief that the spell of that moment had been broken. Because this also was true. She *was* royalty; but it was the forest that was her realm, and she its queen.

Everyone began to chatter – trying to soothe her, declare their love for her, show their gratitude to her.

'The huntsman entrusted you to the wolves long ago and we've watched over you ever since,' said Tobias warmly.

'You were the sweetest little thing I'd ever seen,' Akina chuckled.

'You looked so lovely in the winter bonnets I made for you,' added Etienne.

'I remember the time I taught you to swim. You took to the water like a fish.' Sailor grinned fondly.

'You made us a true family,' Jeremiah whispered, his tears falling into Wisdom's fur.

Wild Rose cut them off. 'Snow is my mother,' she said, locking eyes with the wolf of white majesty, 'and you are my family. I care not about the queen. I only want to set Aurelia free.'

'You cannot go to the castle again,' warned Tobias, Rogue howling in agreement at his side.

Wild Rose stared at him defiantly, but the mother bear came to her side, reached up gently and took her hand. 'You have such courage,' she said quietly. 'My name is Sophia. This is my husband Winter and our daughter Hester, who you know. We are so grateful to you for uncovering the truth about the curse.'

To Wild Rose's astonishment, Sophia kissed her hand.

Winter came and knelt before her. 'Now that we know the curse isn't real, we will rescue our daughter from the castle. We had a plan in place for many years – the Rising. Now finally, at the Midwinter Ball, we will save our daughter and bring her home.'

Wild Rose said nothing. She had known her family would have a plan; they always did. And perhaps their idea would work – who was to say? But it was not going to stop her, Aurelia and Saffy conjuring their own cunning scheme.

'The queen will invite every boy in the land to attend the Midwinter Ball,' Sophia began.

'Someone will be chosen to be Aurelia's future husband and the betrothal will happen that night at the stroke of twelve,' Winter continued.

'All we have to do,' said Oak conspiratorially, her bright eyes flashing, 'is get the queen to choose our boy.'

'Which boy?' asked Wild Rose.

'The boy who dwells by the Hidden Lake,' murmured Riven. 'The one whose brother you saved.'

'The one who makes the fancy shoes!' exclaimed Etienne with a dreamy expression.

Wild Rose knew exactly who they meant: Jack Willows.

'On the night of the ball, our boy will present the princess with such an exquisite pair of shoes the queen will have to approve the match,' said Jeremiah with a wink, taking Etienne's hand.

Wild Rose frowned and Akina read her thoughts. 'The shoes shall be quite spectacular. We've been saving jewels from the mine, all the queen's favourites: sapphires and diamonds and moonstones. They will be like nothing you've ever seen.'

Wild Rose nodded, certain that Jack and his family were capable of creating truly enchanting slippers.

'Once they are betrothed, Aurelia will have more freedom,' said Oak, grinning. 'The queen will soften her grip, knowing that "the curse" can be broken but the princess is still in her control. The Willows boy will invite her to his home to visit his family and that's when we'll strike!'

A wild cheer, raw with hope, rang through the glade like a victory call.

Only the Lady Mal remained silent, her face masked by shadows.

'We'll ambush the Royal Guard,' growled Tobias, 'and set the princess free.'

'Her guardswomen, one of whom is my sister, will take the princess away to safety,' explained Winter.

'But really they will give her to us, and we will take Briar away from here,' Sophia said firmly, 'and find somewhere safe.'

The mission was set. And, with that, Wild Rose bid her family farewell, whistled softly to her wolves and rode away. Two plans would unfold upon the very same night. There was no doubt that Aurelia would be freed. And, in Wild Rose's mind, no doubt which plan would succeed.

There was much still to do.

Past the oak tree with the old rope swing she cantered on the little grey horse, out of the treeline that was her safety, towards the walls of the Ebony House.

The heady scent of lilac and camomile reached her and Wild Rose breathed in deeply, feeling encouraged by the garden's floral magic.

Dismounting, she tethered the horse to the post of the tumbledown gate and crept through it, heading for the large oak door.

As Wild Rose approached, the door flew open and Saffy came dashing out with her snowflake cloak again thrown over her nightgown.

'Wild Rose! What are you doing here?' she asked, looking concerned. 'Has the plan changed?'

'No,' Wild Rose said, trembling.

Saffy reached out and took her hand as the words fell from Wild Rose's lips. 'The queen is my mother. She wanted to drown me, but your father saved my life.'

Saffy threw her arms round her friend and they stood that way for a long moment.

'Did you know?' asked Wild Rose softly.

Saffy shook her head, taking in Wild Rose's elven beauty and suddenly seeing the star-bright likeness to the queen.

'I knew you were born in the castle, but not to the queen.'

Lullaby emerged out of the shrubbery and Snow leaped over the gate. But Saffy didn't flinch. She just stared at her friend encouragingly, still holding her hand.

'Would you like to speak with my father?'

'Yes,' Wild Rose whispered.

And so, for the first time, Wild Rose stepped into a home beyond her realm. So many different scents seemed to mingle in the air: an oven filled with baking bread, long-boiled peach tea going cold in the corner, the spilled blood of a freshly killed rabbit and the wooden smell of the house itself. The warmth and liveliness of it might ordinarily have overwhelmed her.

But her heart drew her across the room to where a magnificently tall man rocked a chubby baby in the crook of his arm.

'Thank you,' she said, 'for sparing my life.'

The huntsman laid a gentle hand upon her shoulder. 'Wild Rose, I could never have left you to die.'

'You were sworn to protect the queen,' she said quietly. 'You must have broken an oath to save me.'

The huntsman nodded gravely and drew her unexpectedly into a hug. The baby protested and gurgled furiously, making Wild Rose laugh.

The huntsman dipped his head to her, almost like a bow. 'And thank you, Wild Rose, for saving my daughter.'

'And welcome to our home,' said a warm voice.

Wild Rose turned to face Ondina, a woman with hair dark as a raven's wing, streaked with silvery grey.

'Come and have some breakfast,' she beamed, and they all sat and sipped mint and camomile tea, and ate fresh bread with glistening damsonberry jam until the sun was fully risen in the sky.

And, though Wild Rose had never felt more welcome, still the room felt too hot and her dress felt too sparse and the cloak felt too heavy. She could not keep from longing to feel the wind on her face. The ice melted from her hair and she had never been so grateful for its cool, damp kiss upon her neck.

When the sky had warmed to a blossom-pink hue, Wild Rose and Saffy walked to the end of the garden and out of the gate; they moved along the edge of the forest until they came to the oak tree swing. Still hand in hand. Wild Rose reached out with the crook of her elbow and untethered the little grey horse.

They sank on to the swing, side by side. Saffy took a piece of parchment and some ink from her pocket and began their letter to Aurelia, Wild Rose narrating, Saffy writing it down word for word.

How the queen had tried to have Wild Rose drowned. How the huntsman had saved her. How the Folk of the Forest planned to rise up. How Aurelia must keep faith in their own plan.

Next Saffy took a well-worn book of winter remedies from the depths of her blue cloak and flicked through until she found what she needed. She tapped a finger on a handwritten recipe.

> *Lavender oil x1*
> *Dried lavender buds x1 handful*
> *Cinnamon curls x4*
> *Pressed camomile leaves x2 handfuls*
> *Lily pollen x1 sprinkle*
> *One large valerian root*
> *Crushed ginger x1 sprinkle*
> *Dried magnolia petals x2*
> *Winter maple flower x1*
> *Single wing of a moon moth*

*Mix the ingredients together and boil with the
thorns of a pink rose and fresh clementine peel.
Flavour with mint or apple-blossom honey.*

'It's a lot to gather,' Saffy mused. 'But I can seek
the herbs in my mother's stock.'

'I'll get the dried flowers, thorns, clementine peel
and moon moth from the forest,' said Wild Rose
confidently. 'Then we'll need to boil it and test it on
someone, so we know it works.'

'Once we're sure, I can use my mother's vials to
take it to Aurelia when Verity and I next visit the
castle.'

They stared at each other hopefully. There was
much to achieve . . . and all in secret!

But they were still two days from the ball. It felt
like all the time in the world, and no time at all.

'And if Jack is to be the one who wins the queen's
approval with a pair of shoes, do you think he needs
to know about our plan?'

Wild Rose considered this a moment. 'Can we
trust him?'

'Most definitely,' Saffy assured her.

Wild Rose nodded. 'Then I will speak to him. One
last thing,' she beamed, her face alight with beauty.
'Do you have anything I could wear to the Midwinter
Ball?'

CHAPTER TWENTY-FIVE

To Catch a Wild Thing

As the wolves, the girl and the little grey horse sped through the sunlit forest towards the house by the Hidden Lake, peace descended upon Wild Rose as her thoughts drifted and danced. She felt dreamy and light-headed and she might even have started to sing, but the wolves suddenly went quiet at her side, the horse prancing uneasily.

Dismounting, she led the little filly off the main path, listening hard. There came the angry caw of two circling crows. The bright-feathered trill of a magpie taking flight. The wondrous swoop of a goshawk's wings as it shot arrow-like into the air.

Birds are always the first warning.

Wild Rose tethered the little grey horse near a secluded patch of thistles, knelt by her wolves, *her family*, and murmured urgently for them to run into the wilderness.

Snow gave a stern growl, nudging Wild Rose with her snout as if to return the caution, before vanishing in a streak of white.

Lullaby gazed at Wild Rose long and hard, her deep gold eyes unblinking in their loyalty.

Go.

Lullaby gave a low melodic moan and ducked into the undergrowth.

Wild Rose leaped into the boughs of a chestnut tree, swinging herself up and moving through the high branches like a girl running on air.

At the lowest point of the river, where the current rounds a sharp bend, a horse was dipping its head to drink. It was the gleaming white of a unicorn, its mane draped in a tapestry of star-spun gold, its bridle edged with sapphires.

Wild Rose went still. If it was the Royal Guard, she needed to flee and warn her family.

But the rider wasn't dressed in a fur-lined hat or berry-bright cape as the castle guards wore. He was adorned in deep blues, like the hues of a snow-capped mountain. His face was stern, almost icy, and he seemed young, maybe only a few years older than her.

He's not a villager or a guard. He is a mountain stranger.

The horse whinnied in agitation, turning its head sharply left and right, startled by the presence of unseen wolves. Wild Rose didn't move, but the stranger looked up, staring over the River Spell and into the trees as if he sensed her.

There was something haunting about the directness of his gaze, and Wild Rose tensed. She was used to observing travellers, but this felt different.

This boy stared at her forest as if he were its king. Wild Rose bit her lip to stop herself from snarling. Then she saw the bow across his back, the many arrows, the sword in its scabbard, and, with a sickening jolt she understood: he was here to kill.

Not my wolves. Not in my forest.

'Jonas, I told you it's just a fairy tale,' came a familiar simpering voice.

Behind the boy was a girl in a cape of spun silver, riding a palomino mare in extravagant regalia. Her hair was a cascade of glorious spiralling braids.

The very same girl Wild Rose had rescued from outside the bears' cottage.

Verity. What is she doing back in the forest?

Around Verity clattered two of the younger royal cousins and Hugo, Aurelia's little brother, also on magnificent steeds and wearing blood-red capes. Capes of the same red velvet as Wild Rose's own scarlet cloak.

The irony almost made her smile, then it hit her very hard in the chest. They were not just royals, they were *her* cousins and brother.

Quickly she pushed the thought away and steadied herself in the tree.

This must be Verity's royal fiancé, Wild Rose realized, studying the older boy.

'I saw her with my own eyes,' said Jonas, speaking in the same sharp accent as the queen. 'She was swimming in the moat by moonlight in a pair of wings. A wolf pulled her out.'

Wild Rose's heart lurched.

'A girl in a pair of wings!' The younger royals burst out laughing. 'You must have been dreaming!' they roared. 'There's no such thing as the Swan Maiden.'

'Exactly,' said Verity airily.

Jonas turned his horse about, regarding the younger boys with an air of scorn.

'I know what I saw and if you're too cowardly to follow me, go home.'

They fell silent.

'Maybe you did see the wild girl,' said Verity, flicking her wonderful braids over her shoulder. 'I've seen her. And her wolves. I assure you – she's just an ordinary girl in a velvet cloak. There's nothing special about her at all.'

'Doesn't matter. She was trespassing.'

And, with a sickening lurch, Wild Rose understood: he was here to hunt her.

'This is the spot where she and her wolves come to drink,' said Verity. 'I've seen them many times. You could set the trap here and return tomorrow.'

Wild Rose frowned. Verity had never seen her drink here; she was not someone who came into the forest at all. So what was the golden girl doing?

Is she trying to protect me?

Wild Rose was stunned.

The mountain prince leaped from his horse, tethered the white stallion to a tree, his three younger cousins struggling to move as rapidly as him.

'We catch this wild thing today,' he said with snide menace.

'As you wish,' Verity sighed. 'But she is wise to the ways of the forest. She will not approach if she sees you first. And she *will* see you first.'

Jonas frowned, seeming to consider this.

In the high branches, beneath the hood of her crimson cloak, Wild Rose smiled. Verity *was* defending her. An unexpected good deed, in return for rescuing her.

Wild Rose watched in mild amusement as the princes wrestled a huge leafy net into the trees while Verity sat by, not lifting a finger. Once the net was secured with thin twine, *almost* invisibly, the four princes climbed back upon their horses. Jonas brought his horse to the riverbank, letting him drink once more as they waited.

'I don't believe she was maimed by a wolf and then lived to tell the tale,' Jonas muttered. 'That's impossible. She must be a witch.'

'No, she really is a villager,' Prince Hugo said. 'Her parents died in a snowstorm and the wolves were going to eat her, but she managed to tame them instead.'

'Think what you like,' said Jonas flatly 'Nothing about that story rings true. I bet she's a sorceress.'

Verity laughed, but her voice sounded strained. 'A witch . . . in Silverthorne Forest? Oh, Jonas, I'm sorry to disappoint you. She's just a filthy beggar girl who lives with a pack of wolves.'

Suddenly there was a howl in the distance and Hugo's horse spooked and plunged into the river, losing its footing in the mud. The horse lashed out as it fell, its hooves pounding the air in panic. Hugo shrieked, high-pitched and terrified, his leg half caught beneath the weight of the horse, cold water closing over his head.

Milo, one of the other royals, ran to help his younger cousin. But Jonas's white horse butted him hard with its broad forehead and, to his horror, Milo found himself toppling into the river too.

And the little prince was still underwater.

Wild Rose cursed. She had sworn never to let anyone drown in her river and she wasn't about to break a promise.

One moment the banks of the River Spell were woods, wind and sky, the next moment a girl in a cloak of scarlet leaped out of the air.

Verity swallowed a gasp, trying not to look stunned. Jonas felt his breath catch in his throat at the marvel of her.

With a single hand, she twirled out of her red cloak and plunged into the water, at the narrowest point of the river, where the horse and boy were trapped, heaving Milo, the older royal, on to the riverbank at Jonas's feet, where he sat, panting, watching in astonishment as she dived beneath the surface, seeming to vanish.

Everyone stared, enrapt, gawping as Wild Rose let her back sink into the river mud while her feet pushed and rolled Hugo's horse up to standing. The second it was on its feet, the animal charged upstream, away from danger.

Wild Rose burst from the surface again, dragging the shivering Hugo to his feet, her arm about his neck as they stood in the thin curve of the river, staring at the boy on the white horse.

Hugo gasped, spluttered and was sick.

Wild Rose held him steady so the current could not steal him away and whispered, 'Don't be afraid. I won't hurt you.'

Then she bellowed at Jonas, 'Leave the forest or you will never see this boy again!'

On the riverbank, Milo struggled to his feet in alarm, sweat and mud running down his face. 'We'll go!' he cried. 'Just please give Prince Hugo back.' And he reached out his arms, almost touching them.

Jonas smirked, as if losing the little prince was not something he considered a problem. Then he sent a set of arrows into the treetops, slicing the thin twine that secured the net. And, in what would only ever be remembered as magic, the Wolf Whisperer scooped the half-drowned prince up and leaped backwards in one fluid movement on to the far riverbank, out of the way of the net.

The net fell fast, its edges weighted with rocks.

It was then that Wild Rose saw a flash of fur slip into the river, a wolf with a coat the same mottled fur of many shades.

NO.

The net hit the surface, its edges sinking to the bottom, trapping Lullaby in its spider-silk grasp.

Lullaby gave a growl that could raise the dead, her teeth gnashing at the net.

Wild Rose struggled to remain composed. She remained motionless on the riverbank, holding the little prince steady, not wanting to provoke Jonas. 'Be still,' she said softly to her wolf, keeping her voice light, making her face go blank. She had dealt with hunters like this before, and she knew you must never show fear.

The river was so narrow – one step and she could have grabbed the net with her own teeth and heaved it off her wolf. But she couldn't risk Jonas attacking; it would only take the white horse a single step and they would be upon the wolf. If Lullaby attacked the boy, either the prince or the wolf would die.

Lullaby gazed at her long and hard, her teeth bared, her deep gold eyes burning with fury.

Be still.

The wolf in the net stilled. Wild Rose's mind whirred. She needed to frighten Jonas away without touching him, and also keep Lullaby calm.

What she needed was a hint of magic. What she needed was a spell.

She observed the hunting party quite intensely, noticing that none of them carried lavender. It was the first rule of the forest, yet no one knew it. Seemingly not even Verity. Resting her little arm on Prince Hugo's shoulder, Wild Rose stooped to reach into the deep pocket of her scarlet cloak, which lay on the forest floor. Her hand met some loose lavender buds that had formed a violet-coloured powder over time. Carefully she concealed the powder within her fist. It was not quite magic – but they didn't know that.

'Release my wolf,' she called, her voice floating high, 'or you will awake one day with the head and heart of a bear.'

Verity quailed. Jonas chuckled dryly.

Wild Rose closed her eyes and began chanting an incantation, the way the Lady Mal had taught her.

> *'When the pink moon sets*
> *And the sun rises fair,*
> *You shall awaken*
> *With the head of a bear.'*

'Let's go,' whispered Verity nervously. But Jonas only stared at Wild Rose and the wolf with contempt.

Feeling the wind at her back, Wild Rose repeated the spell and this time, for effect, she raised her fist to the sky, tossing the lavender powder high into the air in a purple arc that sailed straight over the river into the face of the white stallion and its rider. As if an enchantment had truly been cast.

Verity screamed. Jonas burst into a sneezing fit. The horse, now with a violet nose, began thrashing its head in alarm.

As if she were roused by the spell, Lullaby finally bit through the twine of the net and lurched halfway out of the water, her furious jaws closing round the white stallion's leg.

Wild Rose gasped in horror.

'No, Lullaby,' she pleaded, but it was too late.

The horse reared. Jonas, part blinded by lavender powder, slipped from its back, landing quite splendidly on his feet, his sword drawn, ready.

He looked at the wolf. Raised the sword high.

Lullaby growled without mercy. Hugo clung to Wild Rose in alarm, as if in that moment he was on her side, willing the wolf to be safe. Wild Rose screamed as the sword came down.

It struck Lullaby's snout, leaving a deep, bloody gash.

Wild Rose let go of little Hugo and plunged into the river, half mad with rage, hurling herself between the sword and her wolf.

Through a violet haze, the prince swung the sword round his head, preparing to strike again.

Verity yelled but covered her eyes. Milo looked away in shock.

Wild Rose flung herself over the wolf. The sword came down, its motion unstoppable, even though Jonas tried to stumble back. Wild Rose closed her eyes and tucked in her head as the blade struck. The tip of the sword sliced at her back, cutting its way through her tangled blonde locks as she and Lullaby tipped into the river.

The hair fell in a twisted curl on to the surface of the water, where it caught against a small rock. But there was no blood.

Jonas stood statue still, sword in hand like a boy turned to stone.

'Get out of my forest and never come back.' Wild Rose's voice was low, like the crack in the universe where lightning lives, parting the clouds before thunder.

Jonas startled back to life, his ashen face streaked with violet. The white horse had long since bolted so Jonas leaped on to Milo's horse, pulling a shocked Milo up behind him.

Prince Hugo, seeing his family ready to leave, moved cautiously back across the water. As he passed Wild Rose and the wolf, standing huddled in the middle of the river, his blue eyes, a mirror of the water, seemed to say one unspoken thing.

Thank you.

She nodded at him.

And he grabbed the pale lock of hair from where it was caught on a rock and pushed it into her hand.

'GO!' Wild Rose ordered, her anger raw enough to summon a storm as she numbly slipped the hair into her pocket.

'Come,' Verity said fearfully, helping Hugo out of the river and up on to her horse, not even caring when he spread mud on her silver cape.

In a pounding of hooves and racing of hearts, they were gone.

Wolves appeared, howling brutally, a song of savage intent. But they did not cross the water. Some stared into the river; others licked Lullaby's snout clean.

Wild Rose stood, drenched and furious, with wolf blood smeared across her face, stoic and fierce. She stayed in that river for a long while, anger pulsing through her veins as she watched the hunting party leave.

No one hurts my wolves and gets away with it.

At some point, the sky greyed and it began to softly rain. Wild Rose came back to her senses and climbed carefully out of the water, nudged by Lullaby. Her cloak at least was dry and she carried it over her arm as she wound her way through the woods, the little grey horse walking beside her, to the glade.

There was no one home and it was easy for Wild Rose to slip in through the Forest Folk's low window, bringing her beloved Lullaby with her. She lit the fire and hung her cloak above it. Then, having doused Lullaby's wound with camomile, she heated some water for a bath and peeled off her wet clothes.

Steam rose and misted the glass, the water warming her skin with its kiss. Wild Rose closed her eyes, her mind whirring with a single burning thought.

We are not safe in this part of the forest any more.

Jonas was one boy. He was nothing to fear. But the queen could send an army.

What would happen when Aurelia went missing? Who would be blamed? The Royal Guard knew the Deep Wood and the Wild Wood.

Sinking further into the warm water, Wild Rose thought of all the folk who dwelt in the forest. And a strange thing occurred to her that she had never considered before.

Everyone in the Silverthorne Forest is different in some way.

Her beloved family, forced to work in the mines for their freedom.

Old Eleena and her son, who didn't use words to communicate.

The Lady Mal, unapologetic and so powerful in her knowledge.

Even the family of bears with their broken hearts had found refuge among the whispering trees.

And in that moment Wild Rose had never felt so grateful to be alive. She would not have swapped a single windswept, frozen night. Because then she might never have known the moonstruck wildness of wolves. Or how a band of banished folk could forge a home with love. Or how to find courage even in the deepest dark. Or cast a spell by starlight. Or cross a moat at midnight.

'The forest is our home,' she said to Lullaby triumphantly. 'And there is much of it to roam . . . We must be ready to explore all of it. The Faraway Wood and beyond.' The wolf gave a little yelp. 'We know it better than anyone! We must be wiser, bolder, wilder.

'If the queen comes looking for us, she must never be able to find us!'

CHAPTER TWENTY-SIX

The Boy by the Lake

Twilight was falling on the third night before the ball when Wild Rose arrived at last at the Hidden Lake. The sky and water were a cloud-spun grey, both twinkling with early starlight, the air misty with the sparkle of rain.

She chose the same route Saffy had taken on the fateful day she got lost. That day had been little more than a week ago – and since then all their lives had been altered by that Girl in the Scarlet Hood. Wild Rose took in every leaf, fern and bramble. Every fallen feather. Every cry of the keening wind. And pressed their essence to her heart, like dried flowers.

Oh, how I love this forest.

Reaching out ahead of her, she parted the leaves, squeezing through, the scarlet cloak trailing behind her like a gown. There came firm resistance, as if the forest had made itself into a doorway. But Wild Rose pushed and the leaves gave way, letting her step on to a lakeshore gilded with winter.

At the water's ice-film edge, quite by chance, leaning up against the tree from which his family took their name, was the charming boy: Jack Willows.

He tipped his hat in greeting, pushing himself up off the weeping willow and ambling over.

'Hello, Miss Rose,' he said with his gentle half-smile.

'I suppose you have heard of the Rising by now?' she asked, knowing that Winter would have visited the lake earlier, and alerted Jack's family to the plan.

Jack gazed at the snow, a little crestfallen. 'I am to try to win the princess's hand in marriage,' he said doubtfully.

The moon rose over the lake, golden light lancing off the ice, making Wild Rose feel more sure of herself. She could always find courage in moonlight.

'Do you know the reason?' she asked him, aware of the risk, but daring to trust him anyway.

Jack shrugged. 'My father didn't fully explain. He knows Winter and Sophia from years ago. Some sort of favour?'

Wild Rose took a breath of the wild winter's night and told him the tale of the two babies. One sent to be drowned, the other stolen. The girl in the woods and the girl in the tower. The two isolated childhoods. The woodcutter's daughter who had brought them together, through wolves and a scarlet cloak. The way Jack himself had passed a swan-shaped letter between them, so they might meet by midnight. How the Rising planned to rescue Aurelia by winning over the queen with an enchanted pair of shoes.

Jack stared at the wild girl. And he remembered the strange sensation he'd had when they met by the wild cherry tree.

She'd reminded him of someone . . . And now he knew who.

'You are so like the queen,' he murmured, quite astonished, then hurriedly corrected himself.

'I mean, you look – you have her beauty,' he said, and this time he did not look down, but kept his eyes on Wild Rose with such a direct gaze she almost blushed.

No one had ever called her beautiful. No one from outside the forest.

'I need your help,' she said, while her nerve held. And in a low whisper Wild Rose told him the plan she and Aurelia had concocted.

By the time she had finished telling him, the moon was fully risen, the iced surface of the lake was a deep indigo, and the stars luminous in their glimmering grace.

Wild Rose was quiet, waiting for Jack to speak.

'As you wish,' he said, smiling at her with such a brightness that she could not help but smile back.

And suddenly, in a heartbeat, all the mistrust Wild Rose had ever had about her own worth was called into the light. She had always been told that the villagers would fear her. She had always thought that her own mother had. She had always believed the lie.

She was not a witch (apart from in spirit). She was not a devil (apart from in cunning). She was not a

Fae (apart from in grace). She was a girl grown up in a forest. A princess wrapped in scarlet. A star hidden behind swathes of cloud. This was all it took for her to glow.

'I will see you at the ball,' she said, her face agleam with inner radiance.

Jack bowed his head and strode away, turning once to tip his hat to her again before he disappeared into his house.

Wild Rose danced back into her forest, light as a dandelion bud. She swirled, glided, skipped and spun, twirling in a spotlight of her own making, her arms rising up on either side as if she might fly.

Wolves prowled in step with her, singing their song of blood and dreams, and Wild Rose had never felt surer of her path. Then a sound reached her and she danced up into the trees, quieting her own song as she listened through the wind.

There it was. The crunch and spin of wheels through muddy ice.

Who would take a carriage off the main track in the dark? Surely not the queen . . . Was she visiting the Lady Mal again?

Nimbly as a squirrel, Wild Rose began to run. Through the high branches she fled until she caught sight of a carriage of stunning wrought ironwork trundling unevenly between the trees.

As she squinted through the lantern-lit dark, she realized it wasn't a royal carriage, and she watched curiously as it ground to a halt before a fallen plum tree.

Wild Rose sank into a low crouch, watching as an older boy, who was oddly familiar, climbed down to move it.

'It's not far from here. I'm sure we're close. My father says it's in a glade with a silver birch tree and a hanging mirror,' came a bright little voice, and Wild Rose grinned to see Saffy leaning from the carriage door.

'A mirror in the forest?'

'So the Forest Folk always have an aerial view of the woods,' Saffy explained.

'Have you met them?' asked the young man.

Saffy shook her head. 'I doubt they'll be too thrilled to see us. Reckon we should go the rest of the way on foot.'

'There's no need,' trilled Wild Rose, dropping to the ground.

The young man drew back, but did not look alarmed. Saffy rushed straight into Wild Rose's arms and the two fell into a warm embrace.

'Wild Rose, this is Virtue Silkthread – Verity's brother,' Saffy said brightly.

Virtue bowed splendidly. 'It is an honour to meet you, Wild Rose.'

'Are you all right? Are the wolves well? Verity told me what happened with Jonas.' Saffy stroked the place where Wild Rose's hair had been cut by the sword.

Wild Rose nodded, shivering a little at the memory.

'That's actually why we're here,' added Virtue, tapping on the door of the ornate carriage. It clicked open and a shamefaced Verity stepped out into the forest, the lantern illuminating her hair.

'I'm sorry,' she cried, approaching Wild Rose rather sheepishly. 'I really didn't think Jonas would harm you!'

Wild Rose stared at her hard.

Verity tried another tack. 'To make up for my foolishness, I brought you a gift to wear to the ball. Saffy said you wanted to borrow a dress, but this you can keep.' And Verity handed over a gown of exquisite dark rippling feathers.

Wild Rose held it up in astonishment. It was supremely glorious, reminding her of cascading waterfalls.

It was perfect.

'And this,' Verity chirruped, passing over a cape the hue of midnight tulips.

A cloak to cast spells in.

Wild Rose could not keep from smiling.

'And lastly these,' Verity added, placing a midnight-blue box in her hands.

Gingerly Wild Rose opened it and her heart almost stopped. For in the box were a pair of shoes cut from magic. They appeared to be crafted entirely from ice, but they weren't cold to touch. They were slipper-shaped with thin heels that ended in needle-like points, refracting the light of the lantern in little rainbow prisms all round the woods.

'Jack made them for me,' said Verity airily. 'But, now that I'm marrying Jonas, I hardly want them as a reminder.'

'This is the most beautiful gift I have ever been given,' Wild Rose gasped.

'I truly am sorry,' mumbled Verity.

'I know,' Wild Rose said softly. 'Will you be taking this carriage to the ball?'

'Yes,' answered Virtue. 'I'll be driving it there and back. Reckon I'll skip the ball and wait with the horses.'

Wild Rose's eyes lit up like stars. 'Would you do me the honour of letting me ride with you?'

'Why, of course!' cried Verity in excitement. 'Saffy's riding with Jack, so there'll be plenty of room.'

'Where should we pick you up?'

'Right here, by the fallen plum tree.' Wild Rose beamed. 'But come a little early as you'll need to help me perfect my costume.' And, before they could ask any further questions, she danced away into the woods.

CHAPTER TWENTY-SEVEN

She Shall Go to the Ball

The next three days were spent in a flurry of whispers and secret plans. Herbs, flowers, moon-moth wings and clementine peel were gathered by nightfall. Saffy and Wild Rose met by the old oak tree swing to combine everything they'd foraged. Together they boiled the Dreamer's Draught in a cauldron near the River Spell, over a fire whose flames were hidden by the trees. The tiny glass vials Saffy had 'borrowed' from her mother, along with a lock of moon-bright hair, were carried from the forest to the Ebony House in Saffy's basket, which was given to Verity, who presented it to the guardswomen as a betrothal gift for Aurelia.

In return, letters were written on tiny scrolls and bound carefully to the legs of doves who carried them over the moat and the Spindle Wood to Saffy, who passed them to Jack on the edge of the Hidden Lake to take to Wild Rose.

A marvellous pair of shoes was made from crystal and sapphire and moonstone. Shoes to win the hand of a princess, and the heart of a cruel queen.

And Prince Jonas struggled to sleep for fear he might awaken with the head of a bear . . .

As for Wild Rose's family, they found that they slept better than ever. Perhaps it was the cold weather that sent them early and yawning to their beds, or maybe the lavender and clementine soup that Wild Rose insisted on making. Wonderful stuff, for after a bowl they would be asleep in moments.

When the day of the Midwinter Ball finally arrived, the entire kingdom was alive with an excitement so fierce it burned.

A few hours before the ball began, as the afternoon sky began to darken, in the glade of alder buckthorn and trembling aspen, beneath the lone silver birch tree, a meeting was held. All of the Silverthorne Rising were gathered, along with Benjamin Willows and his sons.

Wild Rose knelt at the edge of the glade with her wolves, her scarlet hood pushed back so she could listen and Lullaby curled at her side. Rogue chewed on wisps of her hair. Wisdom fondly licked her face. Snow was circling the glade, prowling stoically. Guarded. Alert. Ready.

'The shoes will win over the queen and, once she agrees the match, Aurelia shall leave the castle,' proclaimed Oak proudly. A sharp triumphant cheer went up.

Jack Willows, set slightly back from the group with his two younger brothers, gave a casual shrug. Wild Rose thought she saw him blush a little at the attention.

'When they travel to the forest to meet Jack's family, as is tradition, we will strike,' called Sailor.

Sophia pushed her bear head up to reveal eyes bright with focus. She cleared her throat nervously. 'And if the queen doesn't choose Jack?'

'Then we will invoke the curse,' chimed the Lady Mal in her nightingale voice.

Wild Rose sat up very straight, startling the wolves around her.

'We will wait for an ordinary evening when the castle is quiet and the king is away in the Far Kingdom,' the Lady Mal continued calmly. 'I will give Aurelia enough of the Dreamer's Draught that she will sleep for a hundred hours, and we will make it look as if she has fallen prey to a spindle.'

Winter and Sophia held hands, gazing at each other with worried expressions.

'When her betrothed kisses her but she does not awake, the queen will become desperate. She will send for me and I will advise letting Aurelia rest in the forest, so a handsome prince might chance upon her and waken her with a kiss.'

'The princess will, of course, be guarded,' explained Akina, 'but guards are no match for our wolves. When night falls, we move in and take Aurelia to the Faraway Wood.'

Wild Rose said nothing, but her eyes drifted to Jack Willows, who gave her the tiniest, most secretive nod. Grown-ups notice very little when they are busy being pleased with themselves.

The meeting rolled on, dark wine was supped and plans were whispered. As the clouds became starry with twilight, everyone began to leave.

Wild Rose stood, as tall and true as a young tree, and quietly walked over to the Willows family. They bowed their heads to her in welcome.

'Good luck, Jack,' she said wistfully, reaching up and placing a crown of acorns, lavender and small dried roses upon his head. 'Saffy will bring the roses. I shall bring the horse.'

'Thank you,' he said with a subtle grin.

Softly she went next to the family of bears. Young Hester sprang forward and gave Wild Rose a hug. Almost unseen, Wild Rose slipped a folded paper swan into Hester's hands inside which was a letter, written on paper pressed from nettles, penned by quill in violet ink, from her sister in the tower.

Wild Rose winked at Hester to signal secrecy, then raised her head. 'She will be free soon, I swear it.'

Tears spilled down Sophia's face and Winter nodded his thanks. They took Hester's hands and, for the first time since they had moved to the forest, went to join the Forest Folk.

Wild Rose turned back towards her family. She moved to each of them in turn, giving them a garland of dried winter roses, their pressed petals red as blood, as she did every year on Midwinter's Eve.

'Happy birthday,' they grinned, hugging their girl tight, and handing her tiny gifts fashioned from the bounty of the woods.

Lastly Wild Rose swept towards the Lady Mal and held out a bangle woven from lavender. 'For luck,' she smiled.

The Lady Mal eyed Wild Rose sharply. 'What are you up to, child?'

'Nothing at all.' Wild Rose shrugged. 'Nothing at all. Just don't drink anything at the ball.' And she twirled away with her wolves, melting into the trees.

The moment Wild Rose was out of her family's sight she leaped on to the back of the little grey horse and sped across her forest to the fire tree at the edge of the Spindle Wood.

Tethering the little filly, she leaned on the bark of the tree and waited for it to give, then she stepped inside its hollow trunk, a lantern glowing at the crook of her elbow, and began to prepare.

First she checked all the supplies. The staghorn crown Tobias sometimes wore if he wanted to scare off any unwelcome villagers. From Verity, the dark feathered dress, the cape and the spellbinding shoes.

The gold glitter made from amber dust stolen from the mine. A long, slim wand Wild Rose had fashioned from the bark of a silver birch. An old bear head she had borrowed from Hester and, lastly, Aurelia's wondrous black wings.

Next she slipped into the dark feather dress. It was as cool as water against her skin, cascading in layers down to her ankles. Grabbing an old piece of twine, Wild Rose bound up her uneven hair and sprinkled on some golden amber dust for effect, pulling the borrowed violet cloak over the top.

She gathered up everything else, wrestled it all out of the tree and on to the back of the little grey horse. The horse snorted in resentment, and Lullaby eyed her curiously from the darkening trees.

'Now all we have to do,' she whispered, 'is hide the wings and bear head by the fallen plum tree, and take you to the Hidden Lake by moonrise.'

The horse snorted and shook her mane, but she did not resist as Wild Rose led her back across the forest, laden down with feathers and velvet. To the house by the Hidden Lake.

Three hours later, a carriage of magnificent wrought iron bumped its way through the wolf-wild woods, and Wild Rose was ready.

At the fork in the forest, where two pathways led to two different destinies, Virtue Silkthread slowed the carriage to a halt by the fallen plum tree, then whistled high and shrill. Listening, watching, waiting for the woods to stir.

At first, nothing. Then it seemed that the air shimmered, the leaves whispered and suddenly a girl straight out of a dream stood before him.

'Your carriage awaits,' he said. Wild Rose peeked inside and gasped at Verity, who was draped in a gown of royal gold. Her hair was loose from its braids, coiled halo-like upon her head, a crown of its own making.

'You look astonishing,' Verity said genuinely, as Wild Rose and Virtue bundled the wings into the carriage, along with the staghorn crown, Rose's scarlet cloak and the bear head.

'It's just how you wanted it,' Virtue announced rather proudly, gesturing to a thick green velvet curtain that had been expertly strung over both the carriage windows, blocking out all light. No one would have any way of knowing if the carriage were occupied or not.

For tonight, the Silkthreads' carriage was far more than a coach. It was a secret parlour, the backstage of a theatre, a place where legends became real.

'It's perfect,' Wild Rose said softly, climbing in so nimbly it almost seemed she floated. Even in the glass slippers.

'I'm amazed you can walk in those!' said Verity, looking impressed. But Wild Rose was used to running through high branches. She had no trouble balancing on her toes.

Virtue began to close the carriage door, but Wild Rose sang out, 'Don't drink anything tonight. Not the wine, nor whisky, nor winter punch.'

Virtue nodded and held up a tankard he'd brought from home. Then he closed the ornate door, geed the horses on and they bounced and rolled away through the late-night woods.

Beyond the midwinter trees, at the end of a garden softly scented with lilac and camomile, Saffy was terrified and excited, and all the things you might expect to feel on the eve of your very first ball.

Her family had not been able to afford a new dress or shoes, so Ondina had gathered her own dress spun from a fabric like spider silk, a wooden tiara set with large stones, and a comfy pair of forest-hare slippers. Saffy's hair was brushed out into dancing curls fixed with dried roses and lavender, the tiara set upon her head. The snowflake cloak had even been scrubbed clean. At her neck she wore a band of lilac acorns, an ode to the forest. In her hands she held a simple posy of dried wild red roses.

She hovered near the gate with her parents, awaiting Jack's cart. He would take her as far as the castle, then they'd part ways so he could join the line of would-be suitors, declare his love for Princess Aurelia and present the magical shoes to the king and queen.

Wooden wheels rolled over snow slush and two shire horses snorted and chewed. Saffy fidgeted nervously. For at the back of the decorated cart trotted another young horse, a mare as grey as morning mist, her dark eyes wide and searching. Her bridle was threaded with lavender and, instead of a saddle, a blanket was draped across her back.

Bow jovially helped his daughter up to the front of the cart where Jack sat. He was dressed in a suit of midnight blue, a white fox-fur cape over his shoulders.

He looked awfully handsome, Saffy thought. But nervous too, and she remembered he was only two years older than her, still just a boy with a huge task ahead of him . . .

Jack smiled warmly and Saffy felt a wave of excitement sweep over her. Then they were off, rolling away from the village and all they knew, galloping towards the stone-cold walls of Silverthorne Castle.

Saffy took a rose from the posy and slipped it into her hair, then handed the little bouquet to Jack. 'Good luck,' she said.

Jack gazed at the flowers, a silvery spike gleaming wickedly among them. Handling the posy very carefully, he tucked it into his cape and gave a tiny nod of thanks.

In no time at all, they were crossing the drawbridge and Saffy was stepping down into a courtyard bursting with a crush of carriages. She gave a fleeting wave to Jack and joined a long line of women heading through an arched doorway.

Ahead of her, she noticed Verity and her heart danced. Saffy's eyes darted around the cobblestone courtyard and she spotted the Silkthreads' carriage. The green curtain masked the window, but Saffy knew who was tucked behind it and she grinned nervously.

It had been hard for Saffy to trust Verity at first. But Verity had been so truly sorry about Jonas hurting Wild Rose, and so desperate to make amends, that including her in their plan had happened naturally. And Verity had amazed them all by going out of her way to help, so that everything was that bit smoother, that bit sparklier, as if she had sprinkled their plan with gold. For, when it came to secret schemes, Verity was actually in her element.

Saffy pushed her hands into her pockets and crossed her fingers for double luck. The night could go in so many directions. She had to trust that luck was on their side.

It's Wild Rose's plan, she thought, trying to stay calm. *And I'd trust her with my life.*

CHAPTER TWENTY-EIGHT

The Wicked Fairy

As night twirled its mists through the sky, Aurelia stood at the window of her tower, staring at the stars that glittered on the moat.

All my life I have wished upon these stars for freedom, she thought. *All my life I have been someone else's daughter.*

'Thank you,' she whispered to the reflected stars, 'for granting my wish.' And she knew then that there had always been something even stronger than magic. Something made from the essence of twilight rain, and the bright edge of moonbows. Something that held the same radiance as sunlight on water. Something as powerful and possible as love.

Hope.

Aurelia was filled with unstoppable, infinite, unshakable hope.

She slipped on a gown that Arabelle had kindly stitched for her. It was pale green, embroidered with waterlilies and edged with pearls. Fixing her heavy silver crown upon her head, she stood before her emerald-edged mirror and smiled fiercely.

The girl who gazed back looked splendid and focused, flame hair spilling over her shoulders like a cape made of sunset. This was a girl capable of changing her own fate.

Carefully she laid the lock of moon-bright hair upon her whalebone dresser, reached under her bed and retrieved her diamond-hilt sword. It matched her outfit perfectly.

'Goodbye, tower,' she murmured, opening her window and signalling for her birds to fly. 'Farewell, birds. Find me in the forest.'

Evie, Ester and Iris, each armoured to the hilt, their visors down, swords clasped, escorted Aurelia from her tower, through the gardens and into the magnificent ballroom. The room was hung with a thousand chandeliers, each draped in strings of pearls and little blue stones from the river, the floor so shiny it could rival the stars. The king and queen were seated upon high-backed, shimmering thrones of silver, awaiting their daughter.

It was here Aurelia would sit to greet boy after boy after boy. Subtly she touched the little glass vial of Dreamer's Draught hidden in the sweeping skirts of her dress.

Tonight I will be free.

But the thought felt so huge that she closed it away, endeavouring with every ounce of concentration to mask the nervous energy causing fireworks in her soul.

She placed the diamond-hilt sword by her throne, and covered her nerves with a huge beaming grin.

In a daze of smiles and nods and polite conversation, Aurelia began welcoming the young men bearing fabulous gifts. She made certain she was not too joyful when gorgeous presents were given, like a gold-dipped peony. And she made a concerted effort not to be offended by the bizarre ones. A zebra-hide tutu, for instance.

'She's not joining a carnival,' the king said with a smirk, while the queen tutted.

The line at last dwindled, until there were just a few hopeful suitors left.

Aurelia's nerves felt raw with anticipation.

Where is the boy? she wondered, her cheeks aching from the constant smiling.

Another charming young man approached, and Aurelia diligently dipped her head in a smile.

He had kind green eyes, dark hair and a rather lovely snow-white cape.

'Jack Willows, of the house by the Hidden Lake. Esteemed cobbler,' he announced, producing the dried roses, their petals the colour of spilled wine.

Aurelia forced her face to be still. *This was him! This was the boy who had to win her hand.*

'Yes, yes. Now where's the real gift?' said the queen impatiently as Aurelia very delicately placed the flowers in the long pocket of her fox-fur cloak.

Jack Willows knelt proudly before them, holding out a silky midnight-blue box.

The king opened the box and Aurelia's heart caught fire. She quite forgot herself and gasped with genuine, jaw-dropping awe. For inside were the most astounding pair of shoes she had ever laid eyes on.

They were slippers made entirely from moonstone, with slim heels carved into the shape of a swan, complete with yellow sapphire beaks and tiny black onyx eyes. The clasp bending round the ankle was made from dove feathers and the toes of the slippers were adorned with rare diamonds shaped like hearts, which sent rainbows all around the room.

The king raised an eyebrow; he almost looked impressed.

'Very good,' said the queen, actually smiling.

'Mother, would you mind if I wore them now? They're quite the loveliest gift I've seen all night.'

For a moment, Aurelia was sure she'd say no, but the king surprised both of them by shrugging and saying, 'What's the harm? Slip them on.'

Aurelia did so with trembling hands and shakily stood, curtsying graciously to the cobbler.

A flurry of violas and violins filled the air. The dancing was about to begin.

Aurelia stared at Jack, hardly daring to breathe. He bowed low and politely asked her parents for permission to dance with her.

'I suppose you may,' said the queen, looking a little displeased.

The swan slippers were agony and her dress made any kind of movement challenging, but Aurelia didn't care.

As she twirled into position, she saw a maiden in a gown that was old but timelessly elegant. It made Aurelia think of the forest at dawn or a lake at twilight. There was something mysterious about it. Or rather about the girl who wore it. Her autumn-coloured curls were brushed out into a halo of their own making, fixed with small dried roses and stems of pressed lavender.

Saffy! Aurelia thought excitedly.

She looked like the queen of woodland magic. Ready to cast a legendary spell.

As casually as possible, Aurelia glanced at her cousin Jonas, who was looking painfully bored. Verity was at his side, adoringly handing him a goblet of wine. Aurelia chewed her lip as Jonas nodded and took a long swig.

He was drinking the wine!

A trumpet sounded, bringing her back to herself. A cello started up, then a double bass, followed by two gleaming harps and a silvery array of flutes. The room cheered and the dance began.

Jack was a nimble dancer yet pleasantly humble, leading Aurelia gently whenever she moved the wrong way. She soon stopped caring about the ache of the shoes or pull of the dress, or about getting each step exactly right, and instead let Jack and the swish and sway of the music carry her round the room.

Behind Aurelia the arched doors swung open to receive someone new. A whisper ran round the room and Aurelia twisted, surprised, as heads began to turn. A girl stood in the entrance, her face hidden by the hood of her cloak. It was cut from the cloth of midnight and was the hue of purple tulips. From inside the hood, ice-blue eyes stared out.

Aurelia went still, quite forgetting the dance, until Jack mistakenly trod on her toe. She gave a little gasp of pain.

The girl in the doorway didn't move at first. She took in the crowd, like an assassin assessing her enemy. Even the way she stood held authority. She was alone, yet with her she carried the presence of a wolf.

Wild Rose. Aurelia's cheeks flushed with hope. *Now she looks like a real queen.*

'Your cloak, my lady?' said a bushy-bearded attendant.

The girl sank into a deeply elegant curtsy, right down to the floor. As she rose, she seemed to shiver as if haunted by the cold, and politely declined the bearded attendant's offer to remove her cape, keeping it closely round her.

On the other side of the ballroom, Jonas lurched to his feet, staring at her hard, as if trying to place her.

'Let's dance!' cried Verity, clasping Jonas's hands in her own.

He staggered towards her and Verity promptly caught him, steered him neatly back to his throne, and carefully propped his head up as he fell fast asleep.

In the shadows at the back of the room, unseen by almost anyone, a woman with the elegance of a nightingale stood, her hands gripping her gown, her face composed. She took in all that was happening and did not touch her drink.

'Who is that girl?' asked the king, squinting at Wild Rose and looking the most intrigued he had all evening.

The queen had gone very still, as if she were trying to remember something. 'I expect she's a merchant's daughter,' she hissed, downing her blackcurrant champagne.

The night swung by and Aurelia danced with boy after boy. Wild Rose drifted round the room. At some point, she passed little Prince Hugo, who stared at her in wonder. Wild Rose winked at him, then whispered into his ear, 'Only drink water fresh from the well tonight.'

Meanwhile Saffy and Jack Willows quietly moved round the room, in opposite directions, glass vials concealed in their sleeves, so they could casually add droplets of the sleeping potion to the wine, whisky and champagne.

Aurelia, still twirling round the dance floor, caught Saffy's eye and nodded. Saffy steadied her nerve and took three slim flutes of champagne to the guardswomen. They refused, as expected. So Jack approached with three glasses of cool water –

flavoured with lavender – which they willingly drank.

When they were certain that every guest had sipped their draught-laden drinks, Saffy, feeling brave, took Jack's hand and pulled him on to the dance floor, spinning and twirling and laughing with merriment.

It was the first time Saffy had ever danced with a boy and her feet felt light as meadow grass.

Aurelia's heart trembled. This was the first signal. It was time to see if the Rising had worked.

She excused herself from dancing and, making sure her swan slippers were on show, approached her parents.

'I should like to marry that boy!' she exclaimed, gesturing towards Jack.

The queen smiled, her teeth too perfect, her eyes too bright, as she took Aurelia's face in her long, cold fingers. 'You shan't be marrying any cobbler,' she snapped, shoving Aurelia into the arms of a tall young man in military uniform.

Aurelia forced a smile, aware of the room watching her.

Just as the next dance began, she paused and gave a rather long but graceful yawn. Verity saw it and her brown eyes widened. Saffy saw it and gripped Jack's hand. Wild Rose saw it and straightened her spine.

This was the second signal. It meant the Rising had failed.

Verity stood and fanned herself a few times, then snapped her fingers crossly, calling Saffy over to her. 'It's stifling in here – I need some air,' she announced, flouncing out of the room, Saffy trailing obediently after her.

But they did not go out through the door. Verity curved round the dance floor instead, passing Wild Rose and giving her a nod.

Wild Rose touched the clasp of her cloak, moving to the grand staircase near the entrance of the ballroom.

A merry tune sprang up, a fast-paced jig of a dance played on the accordion.

Aurelia curtsied to the man in military uniform, then hurried back to her parents. 'Let's make a toast,' she beamed. 'That I will find my perfect husband by midnight.'

She reached out for their champagne flutes and went to fill them, ever so quickly adding drops from the vial she clutched in her hand.

The music evaporated into silence.

'A toast to our beautiful daughter,' King Aspen boomed. 'May she find a worthy husband!'

'May the curse be broken!' cried the queen, her voice high and a little odd.

Everyone cheered wildly. Saffy and Verity melted into the shadows, giving Wild Rose space.

Then Wild Rose slipped the cloak from her shoulders. For a moment, nobody noticed her difference, the Mark of the Witch eclipsed by her splendour, but then the crowd gasped. The gold dust from the mine made her shimmer, so in the candlelight her skin had a golden-green sheen.

Upon her head was a staghorn crown. She glided forward and, with a shake of her shoulders, two huge wings arose at her back like a bird preparing to fly. In her outstretched hand was a fearful wand, glinting with forest magic.

The dark fairy was among them.

The queen had turned very pale. The king was frowning intently.

The entire room was focused upon Wild Rose, so no one noticed Aurelia dart towards the throne and pull the posy of red roses from her cloak pocket, pressing her finger to the sharpest point. Nodding at Wild Rose in earnest.

Wild Rose sang out in the voice of enchantments. 'You did not heed my warning. The princess shall prick her finger and fall into a dreamless sleep.'

Swords were drawn and the three guardswomen sprang forward. But a scream, high and wild and pure, rent the air and everyone turned to Aurelia, who held the spindle up for all to see. Three drops of crimson blood splashed upon the starry floor.

The world became quieter than a dawn of new snow. Aghast faces peered up at her. Folk drew back in horror. The queen made a terrible retching sound. The king seemed dazed, then gave a bellow of fury. And Aurelia was falling, slipping from the world.

Evie, Iris and Ester came running, gasping at the sight of the fallen princess. The queen clutched her throat. The king drew his sword, then dropped it. The entire room seemed to melt to the floor.

Wild Rose began to brightly sing a lullaby of wolves and lost children. A call to the freedom of the forest. A song of secrets and hearts. Of deep rivers and midnight journeys. Stolen babies and sleeping spells.

No one would remember the words, as she sang in the language of the Fae. But everyone understood that the curse was true and real. Softly they all fell under her spell.

CHAPTER TWENTY-NINE

A Change of Fate

Ester wilted slowly to the ground, her sword clattering loudly on the stone. Evie tried to catch her, but her arms had gone limp. So instead she curled up beside her. Iris laughed in alarm and then slid to the floor.

'What is happening?' asked the queen, but her husband had become glassy-eyed, vacant.

Hugo was staring around the room, quite horrified.

The queen seemed to shiver as if she were made of smoke. 'It's the curse,' she gasped, shaking her head. 'But . . . it's not . . . real,' she murmured – and then she fainted, crumpling on to her throne.

Around the ballroom people had sunk softly to the floor. In the kitchens, in the courtyard, in the chambers, it was the very same scene.

For Princess Aurelia had been so keen to help with preparations for the day that she had demanded that Ester let her visit the kitchen, implored the cook to allow her to decorate the cake, added a dash of Dreamer's Draught to flavour the winter punch, made little pots of mulled wine to be shared with everyone working in the palace, as a special treat to drink in secret during the ball.

As Aurelia lay still as death on the starry floor, the people of Silverdel slumped in sleep over tables and chairs, and all across the ballroom a steady hush descended. Until there was nothing but breath and time.

Wild Rose locked eyes with Verity, Saffy and Jack and they smiled, not quite daring to laugh.

Prince Hugo stepped towards them rather nervously, almost on the brink of tears. Wild Rose went to him, slipped her arms free of the feathered wings and took his hand between her own and her little arm.

'Do not be afraid,' she said as lovingly as if she were conversing with a wolf. 'The spell will lift in three days and all will awaken.'

Hugo gazed at her, lips trembling. 'How do you know?'

'I cast the spell,' she grinned.

'With my help,' said Aurelia, sitting up and almost startling the little prince out of his skin.

'And mine!' chirruped Saffy.

Verity fanned herself coyly. 'And mine, of course.'

The flame-haired princess rose to her feet, and the wolf-hearted girl leaped towards her.

'We did it,' Aurelia murmured as they threw their arms round each other.

Saffy, Verity, Jack and Hugo came to them, their voices low – as if a whisper might awaken the sleeping kingdom.

'This girl is not your sister,' Wild Rose explained to Hugo, gesturing to Aurelia.

He drew back, afraid, confused.

'It's true, Hugo. Wild Rose is your true sister. The queen tried to have her drowned as a baby, then stole me instead.'

'Why?'

'She really did believe me a witch.'

'And are you?'

Wild Rose laughed, low and wonderful. 'Not yet.' She drew him close, holding his hand, but staring also at Verity. 'When you are rulers, promise me this: you will never fear anyone who is different. You will be kind to all. You will lead kingdoms that are places of welcome.'

Verity nodded and Prince Hugo put his hand to his heart. 'I swear,' he said solemnly.

Aurelia turned to Wild Rose and her little brother. 'The throne is rightfully yours, Hugo. Make sure Jonas doesn't get there first.' Her tone was heavy with warning.

He nodded, but gazed at Wild Rose. 'It's rightfully yours, though, isn't it?'

Wild Rose laughed softly. 'I am already queen of the forest. That's my home.'

The clock in the corner began its golden chimes.

'We must go,' Jack said urgently. 'We're not safe here.'

Verity hurried to the corner of the room where the bear head was hidden under a pile of cloaks, and Wild Rose's face lit up! With a wink at Hugo, she crept towards the sleeping Prince Jonas, and stealthily placed it over his face.

'Where is the Lady Mal?' asked Aurelia, looking around suddenly.

'She must have been wise to our plan.' Wild Rose sighed, realizing you could never outwit the apothecary. 'You leave first in the carriages,' she urged Verity, Saffy and Jack. 'Aurelia and I will follow on my horse.' She draped the dark cloak over Aurelia, quite disguising her. Then she laid the wings over Aurelia's throne along with the staghorn crown.

A final gift from a wicked fairy.

Hugo watched her quietly, lingering near the throne. Wild Rose went to him and gently took his hand, looking her younger brother in the eye. Her brother . . .

'Hugo, if you don't want to stay here on your own, you can come to the forest with us this very night. And return in three days.'

Hugo gaped at her. 'Stay with the wolves?'

Wild Rose smiled, nodded. Same blue eyes. Same pale hair. But Hugo looked unsure.

'You would, of course, be most welcome to stay with us,' Verity suddenly cooed. 'My brother Virtue could teach you how to wield a sword – he's awfully good.'

Hugo gave a shy nod. He let go of his sister's hand and moved to stand beside Verity.

The clock reached its twelfth chime and everyone moved as one towards the door. Verity, Hugo, Saffy and Jack hurried out first, sending the guards and waiting coach drivers inside to safeguard the king and queen, or carry the sleeping children home. In the commotion, no one noticed a girl in a gown of dark feathers and a maiden draped in a velvet cloak, her long red hair hidden entirely, slipping from the side door and climbing on to a dusky grey horse.

Verity helped Hugo into the carriage and tossed Wild Rose her scarlet cloak as Saffy climbed into the cart with Jack.

Wild Rose whirled the cloak round her and became the Wolf Whisperer once more. 'To the forest,' she said, and Aurelia's face lit up.

The carriage and cart rattled away. The clouds rolled back to reveal the stars. The moat shimmered dark and deadly. And the little grey horse galloped over the drawbridge, straight towards the future.

Nobody noticed them go.

At the edge of the woods a glass-like slipper fell, to lie in wait for a prince to later find. Then all would know for certain that something magical had occurred.

It was only when they broke the line of the forest, crossing into a world of wilderness and wolves, that they threw their heads back and howled, full of joy and glory.

Wild Rose guided her horse effortlessly through the dark, along the banks of the River Spell and into the woods, her wolves running alongside them. Aurelia was struck with wonder, her hood thrown back, her flame-coloured hair spilling into the night. And Wild Rose laughed delightedly, her blue eyes shining with pride.

'The curse is broken, but the fight isn't over,' Wild Rose said, sounding a note of caution. 'But for tonight, Briar, let's go and meet your true family.'

'I'm ready,' Aurelia said, and they raced on together through the Wild Wood.

Somewhere a nightingale trilled through the sky and, ahead of the girls, a demon horse rode into the clearing. The apothecary reached up and rang the warning bell, her face alight with wonder.

The glade filled with a band of fierce men and women and a family who once were bears.

'What's happened?' asked Sophia nervously, Hester clutched tight in her arms.

'She's done it,' the apothecary said, tears spilling down her cheeks.

'Who's done what?' cried Tobias, eyes wide with alarm.

'Did the queen choose Jack?' Winter whispered, his hand over his heart.

The Lady Mal shook her head, smiling through her tears.

'Our plan did not succeed, but Wild Rose's did. She became the wicked fairy. She broke the curse and freed the princess, and the castle sleeps. Briar is free.'

Then the night was full of cheering and shrieking and hugging and hope.

Soon the little grey horse rode into a scene of wild celebration, carrying a girl in a scarlet cloak and a princess who had dared to change her own fate. Wild Rose was caught by loving arms and lifted into the air, embraced tightly by family, smothered with kisses and beards, cheeks and tears. She laughed brightly and swept Aurelia off the grey horse, leading her over to the family who once were bears.

Hester ran forward, unable to contain her excitement a moment longer. Her eyes were wide with triumph. Winter and Sophia were behind her, clasping each other's hands, hardly able to believe that their long-lost child had returned.

'This is your daughter,' Wild Rose said, with such quiet grace that the forest fell still. Even the wind ceased its song, as beneath the lone silver birch tree a family was reunited. With joyful hearts they embraced.

A wolf white as bone stepped into the glade howling with heartfelt anguish.

Wild Rose fell to her knees, calling back softly in apology, kissing Snow's snout. 'I will never leave the forest again,' she promised the wolf and her family. 'This is my mother,' she announced to all who were assembled there. The wolf bared her teeth. The queen of a thousand winters.

Then Wild Rose stood up and told the tale of the wicked fairy and how everyone had helped her make the rescue possible.

How the queen, the king and the kingdom would sleep for three days. How everyone here was free to leave for the Faraway Wood.

Soon Jack and Saffy arrived, with their families, followed by a carriage of ornate wrought iron carrying Verity, Hugo and Virtue. And, for the first time, the Forest Folk welcomed all the village into their glade for dancing and songs and supper.

Wild Rose and Aurelia smiled at each other across the glade. It was the best birthday either of them had ever known.

Tomorrow they would depart by boat, horse and carriage, carrying lengths of willow wood and cambric coverings to make camp. They would become a travelling band, living freely in the forest, from here to the Faraway Wood and beyond, telling tales by firelight and playing music beneath the stars.

But tonight they would cherish their newfound freedom.

Sweeping trees leaned down in greeting. Wolves prowled and howled. Moonlight coloured the river gold and a wind whipped up the air, whispering a promise of spring.

EPILOGUE

Wilder than Midnight

On the cusp of a fathomless forest stands a castle cold as bone. A castle steeped in grief, since its princess disappeared and the kingdom fell prey to the spindle's curse.

When the queen awoke from her slumber, she was wild with rage. She rode into the forest herself with an army of guards, in search of her beloved daughter.

But a forest can hold many secrets. Promises murmured beneath a new moon. Pathways so twisted they defy any map. Dark truths hidden in the heart of a wolf. There are many strange tales that weave through a wood, and Silverthorne Forest was no exception.

It seemed some terrible work of witchcraft had befallen the woods. For the queen's trusted apothecary had also vanished. The miners who had worked for the queen in return for safety had abandoned the mine, without stealing a single gem. Their home in the thick of the Deep Wood was burned to a cinder. Had they perished? Run away? Been taken prisoner?

The queen searched then for the wolves that she had thought would imprison them. She searched and scowled and screamed, but there was not a wolf in sight. Next she found a cottage, completely deserted but for three bowls of porridge. The queen rode back to the castle, bereft and incensed, but also haunted by the thought of her lost daughter alone in the midnight forest.

Some say a dragon swooped down from the star-dazzled skies, its fiery kiss waking Aurelia, her slipper falling from her foot as the wicked creature carried her away. Others speak of a wolf white as snow, lips of savage red, teeth as sharp as diamonds. They say it was the wolf's swift kiss that broke the curse, and the wolf pack that stole the princess away into the forest.

But Prince Hugo is certain it was the Girl in the Scarlet Hood. A wild sister from the forest. A girl who runs and sings with wolves. He claims it was her kiss that broke the curse, and the princess chose to leave with her, riding into the night on a horse the colour of mist.

Jonas even agreed with him. He was still cowering in fright after awakening with the head of a bear. The queen slapped her nephew hard on hearing such nonsense.

'Of course you don't have a cousin living in the woods!' And she forbade them from speaking such lies again.

But at last she climbed the spiral stairway to her daughter's lonely tower room, noticing how cold and removed from the rest of the kingdom it felt. All the birds were gone and the shutters were wide open, and upon the whalebone dresser was a single lock of moon-white hair. The queen swayed. Her blue eyes glassy. Her skin deathly pale.

'But that child died,' she hissed in a high, strangled voice, and locked the tower shut forever more.

The king was furious about his daughter's kidnapping and charged round the neighbouring kingdoms, keen to start a war with anyone who had seen his lost child. But none had. When he heard the rumour about her leaving with the wild girl, he laughed darkly. He had always secretly believed there was magic in the woods. For many nights, while the queen was pacing the moonlit corridors of Silverthorne Castle, the king took a lantern and rode into the forest. Searching for the Fae, good or bad. He never found them.

The three guardswomen left the castle, heartbroken, or so they say. Guards and cooks and washermaids came and went, Prince Hugo grew into a young man, but the castle remained haunted by rumours and myth. Beyond the castle, in the villages, folk whisper and sing of the scarlet-hooded girl with her band of merciless wolves. Though wolves are a much rarer sight these days.

The forest itself is wilder, unmapped and impassable. Yet sometimes at the turn of midnight, as boats make their way along the River Spell, bright fires crackle and burn, wolves howl distantly and they say, when the wind is high, you can hear singing in voices bright as bone.

At the edge of the woods, somewhere between the wild and the light, stands a house as dark as ebony, its garden sweetly scented with camomile and lilac. On nights when the lone pearl moon is high in the sky, a young woman in a snowflake cloak slips from the doorway and tiptoes into the forest.

She needs no light; she carries no bow or knife. Yet she is never afraid or alone. Night birds fly down in greeting; the trees part their tangled branches. A boy from the house by the Hidden Lake comes to join her and they walk hand in hand, hearts beating with rising hope for a glimpse of a white wolf and a girl made of moonlight and bone.

ACKNOWLEDGEMENTS

riting this book has been a long-held dream, gradually unfurling like the wildest of roses. A story that felt new and shiny and urgent but which seemed like it had been in my heart for all time, slowly preparing to blossom.

There are so many brilliant insightful people who have made *Wilder than Midnight* real. The list of thank-yous is as long as a rope of hair hidden in the heart of a deep dark forest . . . This is my attempt to recognize everyone's unique and dazzling brilliance.

My much-loved agent Claire Wilson, who can see the magic spark of an idea, even if it's shrouded in mist. Thank you for getting so excited about Wild Rose (and finding a home for the story SO quickly).

Naomi Colthurst, thank you for loving this story from the beginning and making my fairy-tale dreams come true in the wildest, wickedest and most wonderful way.

My many glorious editors, who brought so much curiosity, care and compassion. Naomi, Natalie Doherty and Ruth Bennett. You each weaved a different strand of magic through my words, making the story stronger, stranger and brighter. Thank you for helping me find my way in the forest.

Dominque Valente and Jasmine Richards, huge gratitude to you for your enlightened, generous and spot-on sensitivity notes; they lift the story off the page and ground it in reality. I am so lucky to have had your nuanced and whole-hearted input.

Nichola Garde (and a big hello to Ava and Eban), sending you so much love and appreciation for such amazing, supportive, enriching inclusivity notes. Your excellence and insight was fundamental in making this story as positive and authentic as possible. Having you as a friend is the most wonderful gift.

An enormous heartfelt thank-you to the brilliant Flavia Sorrentino for such magnificent illustrations. You have captured the essence of the world so beautifully and brought the three beloved heroines to life in every colour of midnight. I am in awe of your wondrous work.

The fabulous in-house art team at PRH for going above and beyond to create something truly astonishing that looks like a real fairy tale. And a special huge shout-out to Sophia for such gorgeous drop caps – I love them!

To all the marvellous authors who were kind enough to be early readers, thank you for loving Wild

Rose and being part of this enchanting and glorious writers' community, and taking the time and care to write such beautiful quotes. A thousand thank-yous.

The biggest thank-you of all goes to my parents who brightened my childhood with a thousand stories, both real and imaginary. And to my daughter Amelie who is my greatest fairy-tale adventure and the wildest rose of all.

Cerrie Burnell is an author, actor and ambassador. During her time on CBeebies she broke down barriers, challenged stereotypes and overcame discrimination to become one of the most visible presenters on children's TV. She has been listed by the *Observer* as one of the top ten children's presenters of all time.

Cerrie is the author of thirteen children's books, including her first non-fiction title, the award-winning *I Am Not a Label; Snowflakes*, which she adapted for the stage; as well as the Harper series, which was selected for a World Book Day title. She also wrote and starred in the play *Winged: A Fairytale*, as well as creating the one-woman show *The Magical Playroom*, which premiered at the Edinburgh Fringe.

In 2017 Cerrie was awarded an honorary degree for Services to Media from the Open University. She is a patron of Polka Theatre and has been an author-in-residence at Great Ormond Street Hospital.

Since leaving CBeebies in 2017, Cerrie has appeared on television in *Doctors* and made the eye-opening documentary *Silenced: The Hidden Story of Disabled Britain*. In 2021 Cerrie joined the BBC's Creative Diversity team as one of their new Disability Ambassadors.

Follow Cerrie on Twitter
and Instagram
@cerrieburnell (Twitter)
@cerrie.burnell (Instagram)

THE BEGINNING

Wait – you didn't think that was it, did you?

Puffin has **LOADS** more stories for you to discover.

Find your next adventure at **puffin.co.uk**, along with:

- **Quizzes, games and apps starring your favourite characters**
- **Videos, podcasts and audiobook extracts**
- **The chance to check out brand-new books before anybody else!**

puffin.co.uk

Psst! You can also find Puffin on PopJam